One Night

2018 Edition

Includes

One Night At The Palace Hotel

One Night In The Streets of Makati

Bianca Mori

ONE NIGHT AT THE PALACE HOTEL

One night can bring the past roaring back to life...

It's the night before The Palace Hotel opens, and the entire city is abuzz with what everyone is calling a throwback to the Gilded Age. Everyone, that is, except Consuelo de la Red. Faced with a destiny picked out for her and a past she just can't forget, she confronts the choices she has made and the man she was forced to reject. When the past comes crashing into the present, will she listen to her duty or give into the urging of her heart?

ONE NIGHT IN THE STREETS OF MAKATI

She's an heiress on the cusp of a life-changing event. He's a regular guy with an unfortunate habit of sticking his foot in his mouth. An engagement party in the midst of holiday-rush Carmageddon Makati brings them together. Will it be an encounter for just one night?

One Night

Updated edition of *One Night At The Palace Hotel* and short story *One Night In The Streets of Makati*

Bianca Mori

CONTENTS

ACKNOWLEDGMENTS

This book was written as part of the #BuqoSteamyReads writing prompt and unwittingly started a chain reaction. Four books and a pseudonym that has a life of its own later, here we are. Thank you Mina V. Esguerra and Justine Tajonera (then of Buqo) for starting the ball rolling, for the bloggers who've read this through the years and reached out to me with their thoughts, and to #romanceclass—the best support group, cheering squad, beta readers and all-around badasses.

One Night At The Palace Hotel

1

BANG! BANG! BANG!

The knocks on the adjoining door were so loud they reverberated through the peach wallpaper, the plush carpeting, even through the doors of the en suite bathroom. Consuelo paused from intently massaging body oil onto her freshly bathed skin, sighed in frustration, threw on a bathrobe and marched outside. The cool air conditioning, a contrast from the swampy bathroom, kissed her skin, raising goosepimples.

"What?" she snapped, flinging the door open. Her mother, Concha (nee Consuelo Blardony, known by all and sundry as Mrs. Concha De la Red), stood behind with her hair in rollers, a look of supreme annoyance on her face.

"Haven't you heard us knocking?" Concha exclaimed.

"No," lied Consuelo. The truth was that she'd hung the bathroom telephone and blasted mp3s to drown out the incessant knocking and calling.

"Well? You're finally out the bathroom. Let's get you done up, Conchita."

"Why do you insist on calling me that?"

Nothing, but nothing riled Consuelo up than being called 'Conchita.' It represented everything that annoyed her. It was her mother's insistence of passing on that quaint old Spanish penchant for odd nicknames, where her male uncles were called 'Chiqui' and 'Patxi' and her grandmother's female friends answered to 'Tiboop' and 'Amparito.' It was the diminutive of her mother's own nickname too, which made her feel that she was nothing more than her mom's Mini Me. It was how her mother insisted on such old-school practices, and how she clung to such old-school beliefs of their family's worth, even when most of their friends and relatives had wised up and got on with the program.

The De la Reds, the Blardonys, and the families of their ilk: they'd peaked in the 70s. Her mom just did not want to accept it yet.

She glared at the stylists. "Let's work in my room?" She turned from the door and swung it closed without bothering to see if the stylists followed. Instead of a satisfying slam it slid into place with a soundless snick. She had to hand it to Benjo and his attention to detail, down to soundproofing the ballroom-adjacent suites (an affectation from the grand peerage houses on which the hotel was modeled)—it was all over his baby, The Palace Hotel, the newest jewel in Manila's skyline.

"Ma'am, your hair's already drying up, we can work--" said the stylist, wielding a hairdryer.

"Can we not have talking, please," said Consuelo. She settled in front of the vanity and closed her eyes on everything: on the glances exchanged between stylist and make up girl, on the richly appointed hotel suite, on the party tonight and why her mother had been more anxious than usual to show her off, and on the inevitable conclusion to the night. Because surely a 'hotel pre-launch-launch' with just her boyfriend Benjo's family and closest business associates was just a pretext for something more, and her mother's anxiety and her own suspicions were raising old fears and thoughts that chased each other in a complex Gordian knot in her head.

And where those thoughts led, eventually, was someplace she did not want to revisit, but could not stop dwelling on, present circumstances being what they were.

2

Chicago
Six years ago

The line to Hot Doug's snaked down the residential block in a pleasant but decidedly more working class part of the city than the Lincoln Park neighborhood Consuelo lived in. She stamped her feet in the chill fall air. The sidewalk cold seeped into her fashionable but seasonally inappropriate flat boots, but she also stamped in annoyance at traveling all this way for hotdogs. Gourmet, Zagat-rated hotdogs, but still.

Blame her homesickness for the whole thing.

She'd woken up in the middle of the night in a panic, tears streaming down her cheeks. She'd been in the US for six weeks and had gone through a rollercoaster of emotions—something akin to the stages of grief she'd learned in freshman psych, but what exactly her emotional stages were signifying, she did not know or understand. Six weeks ago she was excited and giddy as she watched Manila recede from her airplane window. After a week in Chicago, she felt brave and resigned, like a soldier facing the great unknown. Then the quiet in her small, bare apartment made her anxious. Then she stepped into her first class and felt lost and out of place. Now she had progressed into a full-on black depression.

As soon as the sobs calmed she went online to speak with her best friend. "I want to go home! This is all a big mistake!" she wailed the minute Cora's delicate features filled the tablet screen.

By the time the call ended, an hour later, Cora had sufficiently calmed her down and bucked her up with typical bluntness–reminding her that wasn't this the plan all along, to get away from stifling parents and monumental expectations? Wasn't this why she went AWOL from school in Manila and psyched her parents out by lazing around for a year until they agreed to college abroad? What was all the emotional blackmail and conniving and ingratiating to the wealthy spinster grandaunt for, if not for this?

Cora's sleep-deprived scowl deepened. "How often have you been out of the apartment, Con? *Except* for classes and groceries?"

"There was, uh, Art Institute last month…"

"Geez, Con, no wonder you're going crazy. Get out of your place, get out of your head. Didn't we make a list of all the places you wanted to visit?"

"Yeah."

"And? Get off Skype and out the door, loser!"

So Consuelo brushed off the list, plotted an itinerary, downloaded directions, put on a coat and boots, and did exactly what Cora said.

The first place on the list was famous Hot Doug's, of which Anthony Bourdain gushed so exuberantly; but she did not realize it was such a long-ass bus ride away. Twenty-two bus stops, she counted. Why did American cities have to be so gigantic? Why couldn't they be sensibly manageable, like Asian cities—like Singapore or Hong Kong? Or Manila, for that matter, where you could stand on a footbridge in Makati and spit on Pasay?

She also did not expect that the square red brick restaurant—sorry, "Sausage Superstore"—would be as popular as she'd been warned. The store was still closed yet already there were probably 30 people lined up before her. She stamped her feet again and groaned.

"Woah there," said a male voice behind her. Consuelo ignored it, quickly learning that if you honestly answered the Midwesterners' reflexive "How ya doin' today?" greeting you could get sucked into a long, uncomfortable small-talk situation. Better be the unfriendly FOB who smiled mysteriously and then averted her eyes instead of yakking with people one did not actually care about.

"You might break a toe if you keep doing that," said the voice. She let out an irritated huff in response.

"That's a pity," the voice pronounced. "Pretty, but rude."

There was something so smug and self-satisfied about the voice, and the way it announced things like it was the authority on everything, that pierced through Consuelo's self-imposed remoteness, making her turn and confront the speaker.

And promptly lose the ability to speak for a few moments.

The accent, pitch and volume had her preparing for a blue-eyed blond jock with a beefy neck and chapped, wind-burnt cheeks; she did not expect the tall Asian with the swimmer's body that perfectly filled in a beat-up leather jacket. He also had piercing brown eyes and a sardonic, self-possessed smile. *Of course.* He had to be just her type.

"Hi. I'm Sam," he said, taking advantage of her shock to thrust a hand and introduce himself. "I take it you're not a regular?"

"What makes you say that?" She did not taking the offered palm.

He put it back into his pocket without missing a beat. "The look of annoyance. If you come here often, you'd know what to expect. See anyone else complaining?"

She looked at the pleasant faces around her and the buzz of good-natured small talk and sighed. "Those hot dogs better be fucking good."

He laughed. "So fucking good you'd want to take them behind the middle school and get them pregnant." She bit down a smile. "Come on. That was a good line, yeah?"

"Only because you stole it from 30 Rock," she said tartly.

His laugh was unperturbed. "So what do they call you, then, gorgeous?"

Was this guy for real? "Excuse me?"

"What's your name?"

She raised an eyebrow, but this Sam guy didn't even flinch. It took her a while to get it. In the Philippines her Spanish features and carefully practiced bitchface put many idiots in their place; even her social equals had known to approach her carefully. This uncouth American-raised Dude-Bro obviously did not know he was being given the cue to go away.

Weirdly, Consuelo found it refreshing.

"Consuelo," she finally answered.

"Cawn-sway-low," he repeated.

"Oh for God's sake, you're butchering it!" she protested.

"It's your name; it's too fucking long."

"It's not my fault you can't pronounce for shit."

He laughed again, easily and un-self-consciously. "Help a guy out. What's your nickname?"

The rosebud lips pursed. "Con."

He shook his head. "Nah, that's not right. Con? Like a scam? Gorgeous, you deserve better than that. I'll call you Sue."

A cheer from the front of the line and a sudden buzz of excitement told them that the restaurant finally opened.

"You won't be calling me anything," she replied.

"We'll see about that," he said, flashing another self-assured grin.

Consuelo turned her back on him, suppressing a thrill in her veins. She could feel his eyes on her as the line inched ahead, a gaze hovering over her body. She should have been irritated, but was finding it hard to summon the feeling.

The line stopped by the window. Pretending to inspect the posters and fliers for roller derby matches and tattoo parlors, she snuck a peek at Sam's reflection. He smiled broadly when he met her glance.

"You're Filipina, right?" he asked. Before she could answer, he explained: "It's the accent. And it's the *pakipot* thing." 'Puh-kee-pote'. "You were just checking me out," he winked. "Ah. There it is. That's the smile I was looking for."

She rolled her eyes. "So you're Pinoy too?"

"Yeah. Well, born there; moved here when I was little. You?"

"Studying."

"Oh? Where?"

"De Paul."

"Nice."

"Where do you study?" He didn't look much older than she was.

"Nah. Taking over my dad's business," he said casually. At the look on her face he added: "I'm taking a few business courses—accounting, stuff like that. Everything else I'm learning on the job."

They finally entered the red brick building. Consuelo stood, dumbstruck at the huge primary-colored menu in front of her, the choices superimposed on hotdog-shaped decals.

"You should decide now before you get to the register," said Sam helpfully.

The problem was that, exactly: there were so many different versions of the hotdog sandwich to get, and so little stomach space. Suddenly she was aware of how hungry she was and how she hadn't had breakfast yet. Should she get something from the regular menu, where the sandwiches were named for people—The Raquel Welch Andouille sausage? Or one of the specials? "Boudin Blanc with Fig Mustard, Double Crème Brie Cheese and Pate de Champagne" sounded promising. Oooh, they were offering the same sandwich that Bourdain had on his show!

"I'll have the Foie Gras sausage," she told the bespectacled guy behind the register.

"How about some duck fat fries? We only serve them on Fridays and Saturdays," he offered. Consuelo hesitated—she didn't know if she could finish them, and she did have to stretch her allowance until her grandaunt's next deposit—when Sam stepped in: "Sure, we'll have that. Add a Virgil Sollozzo too."

"Hey, don't—" said Consuelo.

"My treat." He paid for the order, got their number and led her to the only vacant table in the place, tiny, with two chairs shoved against a wall declaring a timeline called 'Critical Links: A History of Encased Meats.' "This way you have to sit with me."

"You're persistent, did anyone ever tell you that?"

"Some," he smiled, settling beside her. The place was crowded and noisy, so he leaned close to be heard. Consuelo could smell his faint soap-and-water scent, study the fine lashes framing his almond eyes, and ponder the shape of his expressive mouth.

"So what's your story, Sue?" he said, his knees brushing up against hers.

"My story?"

"Yeah. You look European but you're Pinoy; you walk around like a duchess but you cuss like a schoolgirl." He winced and tried an apologetic smile. "Jeez, that sounded like a Bon Jovi song."

"A schoolgirl?"

A naughty gleam appeared in his eyes. "Every time you say a bad word you look a little excited."

"Is that so?" she countered, even as she flushed a little at the look he was giving her.

"It is decidedly so." He leaned a little closer to study her face. He watched her mouth, and then his eyes dropped to her long neck.

"You quote Magic Eight Balls too, I see," she said, checking his gaze. They'd just met, but she got the unnerving feeling of him seeing right through her—not in the sense of being undressed by his gaze, but more of someone who was really curious about her, and just her: not her last name, or where she went to school, or who her grandfather was.

Their orders arrived. One look at the hulking plate of golden brown French fries cooked in rendered duck fat made Consuelo glad this guy Sam was with her.

"OK, I want to see this historic moment," he said. "I want to witness your very first bite of a Hot Doug's sausage."

Looking him squarely in the eye, she took a bite. She may have done it a little too provocatively, and she may have enjoyed the sudden hunger flaring in his own eyes—somehow it did not seem like he was thinking about his own sandwich right now—but all that was chased away by the sudden party going on in her mouth. The duck sausage was salty and crisp and juicy, and the foie gras was seductively rich and soft. Everything melded together so sinfully she had to shut her eyes and gasp.

When she opened them, Sam had that maddening smile again, but there was heat in his eyes and his teeth raked his bottom lip. "Told you it was that good."

She took another bite, savoring it slowly, feeling the stirrings of comfort that only a good meal on a very bad day could bring. "You're absolutely right," she said.

"Stick around with me, Gorgeous. I'll never steer you wrong," he nudged the fries toward her.

She popped one in her mouth and had to stop herself from swooning. "Right again, Sam."

He placed his hand over his heart. "My name on your lips—I could get used to that."

"I bet you say that to all the girls." He probably did, too, but she didn't care. The fries were too good, and the foie gras sausage looked a little lonely; it needed her attention.

"Come for a walk with me after this and find out for yourself," he said.

"Have a French fry," she answered, pushing one into his mouth and fighting a giggle when his lips lingered on her finger.

They did go for a walk after the meal. The next day, he met her at De Paul. They kissed some days after that. And after that, well.

She was happy, then. For a whileThe line to Hot Doug's snaked down the residential block in a pleasant but decidedly more working class part of the city than the Lincoln Park neighborhood Consuelo lived in. She stamped her feet in the chill fall air. The sidewalk cold seeped into her fashionable but seasonally inappropriate flat boots, but she also stamped in annoyance at traveling all this way for hotdogs. Gourmet, Zagat-rated hotdogs, but still.

Blame her homesickness for the whole thing.

She'd woken up in the middle of the night in a panic, tears streaming down her cheeks. She'd been in the US for six weeks and had gone through a rollercoaster of emotions—something akin to the stages of grief she'd learned in freshman psych, but what exactly her emotional stages were signifying, she did not know or understand Six weeks ago she was excited and giddy as she watched Manila recede from her airplane window. After a week in Chicago, she felt brave and resigned, like a soldier facing the great unknown. Then the quiet in her small, bare apartment made her anxious. Then she stepped into her first class and felt lost and out of place. Now she had progressed into a full-on black depression.

As soon as the sobs calmed she went online to speak with her best friend. “I want to go home! This is all a big mistake!” she wailed the minute Cora’s delicate features filled the tablet screen.

By the time the call ended, an hour later, Cora had sufficiently calmed her down and bucked her up with typical bluntness–reminding her that wasn’t this the plan all along, to get away from stifling parents and monumental expectations? Wasn’t this why she went AWOL from school in Manila and psyched her parents out by lazing around for a year until they agreed to college abroad? What was all the emotional blackmail and conniving and ingratiating to the wealthy spinster grandaunt for, if not for this?

Cora’s sleep-deprived scowl deepened. “How often have you been out of the apartment, Con? Except for classes and groceries?”

“There was, uh, Art Institute last month…”

“Geez, Con, no wonder you’re going crazy. Get out of your place, get out of your head. Didn’t we make a list of all the places you wanted to visit?”

“Yeah.”

“And? Get off Skype and out the door, loser!”

So Consuelo brushed off the list, plotted an itinerary, downloaded directions, put on a coat and boots, and did exactly what Cora said.

The first place on the list was famous Hot Doug’s, of which Anthony Bourdain gushed so exuberantly; but she did not realize it was such a long-ass bus ride away. Twenty-two bus stops, she counted. Why did American cities have to be so gigantic? Why couldn’t they be sensibly manageable, like Asian cities—like Singapore or Hong Kong? Or Manila, for that matter, where you could stand on a footbridge in Makati and spit on Pasay?

She also did not expect that the square red brick

restaurant—sorry, "Sausage Superstore"—would be as popular as she'd been warned. The store was still closed yet already there were probably 30 people lined up before her. She stamped her feet again and groaned.

"Woah there," said a male voice behind her. Consuelo ignored it, quickly learning that if you honestly answered the Midwesterners' reflexive "How ya doin' today?" greeting you could get sucked into a long, uncomfortable small-talk situation. Better be the unfriendly FCB who smiled mysteriously and then averted her eyes instead of yakking with people one did not actually care about.

"You might break a toe if you keep doing that," said the voice. She let out an irritated huff in response.

"That's a pity," the voice pronounced. "Pretty, but rude."

There was something so smug and self-satisfied about the voice, and the way it announced things like it was the authority on everything, that pierced through Consuelo's self-imposed remoteness, making her turn and confront the speaker.

And promptly lose the ability to speak for a few moments.

The accent, pitch and volume had her preparing for a blue-eyed blond jock with a beefy neck and chapped, wind-burnt cheeks; she did not expect the tall Asian with the swimmer's body that perfectly filled in a beat-up leather jacket. He also had piercing brown eyes and a sardonic, self-possessed smile. Of course. He had to be just her type.

"Hi. I'm Sam," he said, taking advantage of her shock to thrust a hand and introduce himself. "I take it you're not a regular?"

"What makes you say that?" She did not taking the offered palm

He put it back into his pocket without missing a beat. "The look of annoyance. If you come here often, you'd know what to expect. See anyone else complaining?"

She looked at the pleasant faces around her and the buzz of good-natured small talk and sighed. "Those hot dogs better be fucking good."

He laughed. "So fucking good you'd want to take them behind the middle school and get them pregnant." She bit down a smile. "Come on. That was a good line, yeah?"

"Only because you stole it from 30 Rock," she said tartly.

His laugh was unperturbed. "So what do they call you, then, gorgeous?"

Was this guy for real? "Excuse me?"

"What's your name?"

She raised an eyebrow, but this Sam guy didn't even flinch. It took her a while to get it. In the Philippines her Spanish features and carefully practiced bitchface put many idiots in their place; even her social equals had known to approach her carefully. This uncouth American-raised Dude-Bro obviously did not know he was being given the cue to go away.

Weirdly, Consuelo found it refreshing.

"Consuelo," she finally answered.

"Cawn-sway-low," he repeated.

"Oh for God's sake, you're butchering it!" she protested.

"It's your name; it's too fucking long."

"It's not my fault you can't pronounce for shit."

He laughed again, easily and un-self-consciously. "Help a guy out. What's your nickname?"

The rosebud lips pursed. "Con."

He shook his head. "Nah, that's not right. Con? Like a scam? Gorgeous, you deserve better than that. I'll call you Sue."

A cheer from the front of the line and a sudden buzz of excitement told them that the restaurant finally opened.

"You won't be calling me anything," she replied.

"We'll see about that," he said, flashing another self-assured grin.

Consuelo turned her back on him, suppressing a thrill in her veins. She could feel his eyes on her as the line inched ahead, a gaze hovering over her body. She should have been irritated, but was finding it hard to summon the feeling.

The line stopped by the window. Pretending to inspect the posters and fliers for roller derby matches and tattoo parlors, she snuck a peek at Sam's reflection. He smiled broadly when he met her glance.

"You're Filipina, right?" he asked. Before she could answer, he explained: "It's the accent. And it's the pakipot thing." 'Puh-kee-pote'. "You were just checking me out," he winked. "Ah. There it is. That's the smile I was looking for."

She rolled her eyes. "So you're Pinoy too?"

"Yeah. Well, born there; moved here when I was little. You?"

"Studying."

"Oh? Where?"

"De Paul."

"Nice."

"Where do you study?" He didn't look much older than she was.

"Nah. Taking over my dad's business," he said casually. At the look on her face he added: "I'm taking a few business courses—accounting, stuff like that. Everything else I'm learning on the job."

They finally entered the red brick building. Consuelo stood, dumbstruck at the huge primary-colored menu in front of her, the choices superimposed on hotdog-shaped decals.

"You should decide now before you get to the register," said Sam helpfully.

The problem was that, exactly: there were so many different versions of the hotdog sandwich to get, and so little stomach space. Suddenly she was aware of how hungry she was and how she hadn't had breakfast yet. Should she get something from the regular menu, where the sandwiches were named for people—The Raquel Welch Andouille sausage? Or one of the specials? "Boudin Blanc with Fig Mustard, Double Crème Brie Cheese and Pate de Champagne" sounded promising. Oooh, they were offering the same sandwich that Bourdain had on his show!

"I'll have the Foie Gras sausage," she told the bespectacled guy behind the register.

"How about some duck fat fries? We only serve them on Fridays and Saturdays," he offered. Consuelo hesitated—she didn't know if she could finish them, and she did have to stretch her allowance until her grandaunt's next deposit—when Sam stepped in: "Sure, we'll have that. Add a Virgil Sollozzo too."

"Hey, don't—" said Consuelo.

"My treat." He paid for the order, got their number and led her to the only vacant table in the place, tiny, with two chairs shoved against a wall declaring a timeline called 'Critical Links: A History of Encased Meats.' "This way you have to sit with me."

"You're persistent, did anyone ever tell you that?"

"Some," he smiled, settling beside her. The place was crowded and noisy, so he leaned close to be heard. Consuelo could smell his faint soap-and-water scent, study the fine lashes framing his almond eyes, and ponder the shape of his expressive mouth.

"So what's your story, Sue?" he said, his knees brushing up against hers.

"My story?"

"Yeah. You look European but you're Pinoy; you walk around like a duchess but you cuss like a schoolgirl." He winced and tried an apologetic smile. "Jeez, that sounded like a Bon Jovi song."

"A schoolgirl?"

A naughty gleam appeared in his eyes. "Every time

you say a bad word you look a little excited."

"Is that so?" she countered, even as she flushed a little at the look he was giving her.

"It is decidedly so." He leaned a little closer to study her face. He watched her mouth, and then his eyes dropped to her long neck.

"You quote Magic Eight Balls too, I see," she said, checking his gaze. They'd just met, but she got the unnerving feeling of him seeing right through her—not in the sense of being undressed by his gaze, but more of someone who was really curious about her, and just her: not her last name, or where she went to school, or who her grandfather was.

Their orders arrived. One look at the hulking plate of golden brown French fries cooked in rendered duck fat made Consuelo glad this guy Sam was with her.

"OK, I want to see this historic moment," he said. "I want to witness your very first bite of a Hot Doug's sausage."

Looking him squarely in the eye, she took a bite. She may have done it a little too provocatively, and she may have enjoyed the sudden hunger flaring in his own eyes—somehow it did not seem like he was thinking about his own sandwich right now—but all that was chased away by the sudden party going on in her mouth. The duck sausage was salty and crisp and juicy, and the foie gras was seductively rich and soft. Everything melded together so sinfully she had to shut her eyes and gasp.

When she opened them, Sam had that maddening smile again, but there was heat in his eyes and his teeth raked his bottom lip. "Told you it was that good."

She took another bite, savoring it slowly, feeling the stirrings of comfort that only a good meal on a very bad day could bring. "You're absolutely right," she said.

"Stick around with me, Gorgeous. I'll never steer you wrong," he nudged the fries toward her.

She popped one in her mouth and had to stop herself

from swooning. "Right again, Sam."

He placed his hand over his heart. "My name on your lips—I could get used to that."

"I bet you say that to all the girls." He probably did, too, but she didn't care. The fries were too good, and the foie gras sausage looked a little lonely; it needed her attention.

"Come for a walk with me after this and find out for yourself," he said.

"Have a French fry," she answered, pushing one into his mouth and fighting a giggle when his lips lingered on her finger.

They did go for a walk after the meal. The next day, he met her at De Paul. They kissed some days after that. And after that, well.

She was happy, then. For a while.

3

"Ma'am?"

A gentle voice shook her from her reverie. The room came back into focus. She was not in Chicago anymore; she was no longer nineteen either. She studied her face in the vanity mirror. Make Up Girl did a masterful job, and the stylist was able to tame her wild curls into a sleek chignon. She matched the brand-new hotel's swank and style. Benjo would, undoubtedly, approve.

"Thank you," she said, dismissing them, and then her mother bustled in, all fuss and excited titters. Concha was already dressed in a pale gold dress, draped expertly to flatter a ripe figure. Consuelo could see that she had busted out the heirlooms for tonight: deep blue sapphires clustered into Art Deco discs on her ears, a rope of lustrous golden pearls down the front of her dress, and no less than three rings flashing on her hands: a diamond-and-platinum engagement ring, a gigantic pearl nestled in pave diamond-encrusted lily petals, and a relatively understated sapphire solitaire on her pinky.

"Oh, Conchita, you look gorgeous! Tisha and Brandon did an excellent job!" She pounced on the two dresses laid out on the bed and held them against her daughter. "What will you go with, dear? The taupe coordinates so nicely with the color scheme, but would that be too on point, I wonder? This emerald one is a tad racy…?"

Consuelo picked the emerald dress and relished the brief flash of disapproval in her mother's eyes. The dress was a rich, jewel hue, rendered in exquisitely fine silk; but it also bared her sternum and much of her back. A tiny brass clasp by her nape saved her from exposure; and though the skirt was long and trailed a small train behind her, it was draped to hug her hips and accentuate her curves.

She changed as her mother chattered. "Well, why not, no time like an intimate party like this to make an impression, though I hope his parents aren't terribly conservative—you never know with the Chinese. Still, it's so generous of him to offer this room; quite nice and all, although I wonder if all the better suites were taken—I had a quick chat with the maid and she mentioned a delightful blue and white room with real antique porcelain vases. Still, it makes sense if his parents were using it… Ooh, Conchita, but it's actually classy!"

"Thanks, Ma," she muttered, sliding her pedicured feet into gold sandals, grabbing a mother-of-pearl clutch and following her mother outside. They emerged into a lush hallway that still smelled of new fabric and faintly of carpet glue. Ornate mirrors hung along the gold damask wallpaper, punctuated with richly polished tables that practically groaned with the weight of exotic flowers.

They walked to the top of the grand staircase, where her mother wrinkled her nose at a fat laughing Buddha set into a discreet alcove.

"I suppose that can't be helped," Concha whispered conspiratorially. "Concessions must be made to the geomancers. But I still think it's a very silly practice. Quite backward."

"Do me a favor, Ma, and try to keep those opinions to yourself?" said Consuelo. Concha's prejudices had an embarrassing habit of coming out of her mouth at the worst moments.

"Still and all, you have to approve of the taste of this place. Very classy. Not at all what I expected, you know, what with what one usually encounters with these people's aesthetic. They went with the interior decorator I recommended, didn't they?"

"I think they went with a foreign firm," said Consuelo.

"Oh." Concha's disappointment was short-lived, however; because at the other end of the hallway approached Consuelo's father Rudy, the aforementioned Benjo, and Benjo's unsmiling parents.

"Tita," Benjo greeted, bussing her on both cheeks and then taking his place beside Consuelo. Both sets of parents filled the air with polite chitchat, air kisses and *absolutely delighted!* tones. Consuelo bore it all with a fixed smile, checking her tendency to display boredom via bitchface.

Benjo adjusted his tie. "So how do you like the place?"

"It's very nice." His fine features darkened for a moment. "It's very… grand," she amended. He thought for a moment, then nodded in approval.

Consuelo watched him as he listened politely to the oldies. He was very handsome, with smooth, angular planes to his face, but she always felt tense around him, even if they had been going out for two years now. His face had a closed-off, guarded quality, like he was adept at keeping something hidden from the world. Still, he was nice enough to her. He could be a gentleman, when he remembered. The lovemaking, though infrequent, was satisfactory. It was fine. She suspected that she didn't set him on fire, either.

Also, she knew that he had a thing for blue collar sex. But as her mother ever-so-practically advised when she found out: "Everyone has their quirks. You take the good with the bad."

He offered his arm and she hooked hers into it, and the three couples made their slow, stately descent down the carved grand staircase. The well-bred murmuring of society types waiting in the ballroom slowly rose to meet them with each step they took.

Benjo's hands felt icy against her skin. "Nervous?" she asked.

A crease appeared between his brows. "Why should I?"

"Nothing."

"You'll be fine, Con," whispered Benjo. "You look breathtaking. Everyone will love it."

The staircase was on the same imperial scale as the hotel. They kept on descending, she kept on hearing the murmurs bubbling up, yet they didn't seem to get any nearer the ballroom.

His free hand squeezed hers. "Please, thank your parents for me. This is the right sort of buzz I want The Palace to have. Rudy and Concha De la Red. The endorsement of one of Manila's oldest families— exactly what I want people to associate with my property."

Consuelo smiled, trying to hide the disappointment she felt. It hadn't been the first time Benjo had spoken of their relationship in business transaction terms. It did not mean she was used to it.

The staircase curved to stop at the ballroom. It took Consuelo's eyes a while to adjust to the scene gradually unfolding before her; and judging from her mom's excited whispers, her parents were as astonished as she was.

Benjo said it would be a 'quiet, pre-launch event,' elegant and genteel, with 'a few friends and close business associates.' They'd been expecting a small gathering with, at most, twenty people. But one look at the crowd told them that what Benjo and the De la Reds considered 'few' and 'close' wildly differed.

There were probably a hundred people in The Palace Hotel's Grand Ballroom. Consuelo felt dumb at not connecting the sounds of event preparations behind the closed ballroom doors that morning with tonight's festivities. (She'd thought it was last-minute construction work).

The preparations paid off beautifully. The gold and imperial red theme was heightened by masses of orchids and exotic flowers forming arches and columns around the room's periphery. The huge triple crystal chandeliers were complemented by strings of delicate amber glass curtains hung from the ceiling. One side of the ballroom wall was pierced by graceful arches, soaring floor to ceiling in regal lines. Twin polished Art Deco screens discreetly shielded the guests' eyes from the service areas and sound system cables.

Consuelo's mother also admired the scene, but in a very different way. The room was a veritable social register of the city's crème De la crème, but without society columnists and upstarts itching to gossip the crap out of every champagne-fueled conversation. Concha sucked in a breath: she was surrounded by the Grand Dames and Titans who had always been, until this moment, a hairsbreadth out of reach from the sphere she occupied. She felt a sudden wave of joy and affection toward her daughter. Darling, clever Conchita! Even her dearest Rudy looked pleased.

Benjo led Consuelo through the room, through a cloud of perfume and rustling silks, of tinkling champagne flutes and the flash of diamonds and pearls, the sharp clack of designer stiletto and gleam of bejeweled minaudiere. Benjo expertly worked the room, deftly accepting praise, offering a compliment, delivering a joke and parrying backhanded observations, Consuelo elegantly decorating his arm. She smiled and nodded and tried to contribute something meaningful to the conversation, but more often than not she only managed a generic comment before someone else swooped in to claim Benjo's attention. She knew what was expected of her, and so did not let go of his arm until the Big Heavies were approached and properly lubricated with deference. She floated along, letting the social niceties flutter around her, gossamer wings on the wind:

"Congratulations, Benjo."

"What a wonderful place!"

"I quite like the effect, don't you think? Anna Karenina meets Philippe Starck!"

"Mm. More English than Russian, I should think."

"So elegant, in any case."

"Tell me, that triptych over the front desk, that's not a real David Stanley, is it? It is!"

"Oh yes, of course, the De la Reds are a very old family." Consuelo's head snapped towards her mother's voice, engaged in conversation with Chat Sabio, the casino maven from Cebu. "Rudy's grandfather was aide to Roxas, and that's where he became good friends with my uncle Sixto Blardony who was then attaché to the Egyptian embassy. Both the De la Reds and the Blardonys, you see, are very similar. Our abuelos left Spain in the 1800s to do business in the colony. No children of friar rape in our bloodline!" she laughed uproariously.

"I met a Blardony, I think—in Australia?" said Chat, delicately changing the topic.

"Ah, those are Tesio-Blardonys, my second cousins. Yes, quite a few of the family migrated in the '80s."

"A very bad time," Chat shook her head.

"Quite. God knows why the fates became so set against us then."

"Mm?" Chat pursed her lips. "Yes, yes, of course, fate plays a factor. But at the end of the day if you work hard and smart and do your homework, I believe you should overcome anything."

Concha blinked twice, looking mildly offended.

Consuelo's eyes were drawn to a woman in a slinky black gown approaching them with a wide, hungry smile on her face. Consuelo groaned inwardly, but met the lady with two enthusiastic air kisses anyway.

One had to always play nice with Alessa Bruckner-Jones: she'd been, back in the day, a rebel Monserrat daughter—in the social pecking order at par with Consuelo's family—but had the fortune of marrying, and then divorcing, the dissolute third son of an English marquess. She kept the impressive last name, however, and wielded it expertly. Media types loved Alessa, and if she loved you, everyone else followed.

"Benjo! Consuelo! What a marvelous party! Do you know, I just happened upon the Ambassador and he was saying that this place is ever so beautiful. How did you manage such a coup?"

"You know me—with a lot of help," Benjo said, with a little cast-down gaze.

Alessa tittered delightedly. "I suppose, you smart man! I do have to say, you pulled out all the stops for this, didn't you? Even the ladies' room looks like a royal boudoir!"

"Thank you," he said, still with the modesty act.

"And what do the parents say?" Alessa began airily. Consuelo felt Benjo's posture stiffen. "It must be such a difference from those little uniform housing developments they've perfected. Where was that last place they opened—Imus, was it?"

Benjo managed a hollow laugh. "Ah, yes; Friendville, that was the most recent. Although Alessa, you might be surprised to hear but that development was a hit—first phase sold out in a month, and there's already a waiting list for the next."

"How nice!" said Alessa. "I'm surprised, frankly; it's so far and I understand the houses are rather on the small side?"

"My parents always say there's a market for everything," said Benjo, turning up the charm. "For the functional and modest, as well as the grand and opulent."

"Spoken like a true Yu," she said. "I'm sure they are proud of you."

"You'll have to ask them," he laughed. "Have I told you about the details of those arches? I think they'll interest you…"

Consuelo zoned out, starting to feel a little chilly in her dress. Alessa seemed to be terribly interested in the architectural details of old English houses that were adapted into The Palace Hotel, perhaps all the better to show off her familiarity with "Baron Fermoy" or "Last I had tea with Lady Monson." A waiter passed, laden with champagne flutes; Consuelo liberated one and threw back half the contents in one gulp.

The action reminded her of a day, six years ago—a day that she had been remembering more and more lately. Benjo and Alessa's conversation flowed without including her, and so she let her mind wander back in time…

"Easy there, Sue! I don't want to carry you home."

"Don't you?" she teased. Sam huddled with her, a blanket wrapped around them as they sat in the great lawn in front of the famous Jay Pritzker Pavilion, a structure of swirling steel where people could catch free classical concerts. It was early fall, warm by Chicago standards, but Consuelo was not used to the nip in the evening air. Sam had the bright idea of getting a box of wine and plastic cups to warm them up as they waited for the music to start. Consuelo had just downed her third glass, feeling the wine go to her head and mix with the permanent feeling of giddiness she had when she was with Sam. She threw her head back, gazing at the crisscrossing silver bars that arced over the Great Lawn.

"Don't those bars up there remind you of pad Thai?" she asked.

Sam laughed. "I think you're tipsy, Gorgeous."

"Am not." She shut her eyes and breathed in deep, feeling happy. They'd been seeing each other for a week and a half now. Consuelo could not deny it. There was something here. Something special. There were a million reasons for her not to keep on seeing him, and the fact that she was a stranger in a strange city and he could turn out to be a serial killer were actually the least compelling of those reasons. But still. She knew that this could all be a fluke, a result of her loneliness, homesickness and rebelliousness. But the fact

was that he made her feel crazy and reckless and giddy and free in a way that she hadn't felt since perhaps that puberty-fueled, awkward stage-hampered, soul-crushing, mind-consuming first crush.

She wriggled into Sam's leather-clad warmth and listened to his deep, steady breaths; so close that his hairs tickled her cheek, so close that she could smell his minty shampoo, and almost hear his heartbeats, and OH! she gasped, as his lips touched her neck in feather-light kisses, insinuating themselves in the corner of her jaw before softly slipping down the side of her long throat, down to the hollow of her collarbone, and fluttering up her neck again, soft, so soft; butterfly wing-beats that tickled and warmed her all over.

She opened her eyes just as he touched his lips to hers, gently and tentatively, more careful than she expected a first kiss from this cocky Amboy could ever be. He looked deep into her eyes for a moment, and in that split second she had seen so much: desire and arousal and more, so much more: something that reassured her that he had it all together, that it was all in his control, and she sighed and let him kiss her again.

She felt him becoming emboldened by her surrender. He tasted her lips, learning the shape and feel of them, his kisses becoming hotter when her breath quickened as he teased one corner, clutching her shoulder tight when she sighed as he licked her bottom lip. Her mouth parted for him and his tongue explored, meeting hers, knowing her more and more. She sighed again, and this time he swept in, the kiss growing deeper and more urgent, commanding and demanding, and she yielded to his passion. Her hands went up to his hair, and his threaded in her curls, their pulses rushing, blood racing in their veins, the kiss heating into a fever.

He broke off first, watching her with rapt curiosity. Consuelo felt clouded with desire and hungry for more of his touch. He kissed the tip of her nose lightly. "I think the concert is about to start," he whispered.

"Fuck the concert. Take me home," she growled.

They walked to the bus stop, unable to keep their hands off each other, the short while it took to cross the street hampered by frequent stops at dark corners and dim benches to get one, two, three more kisses in; in the bus they huddled together and discovered secret, fumbling ways towards each other's bodies; their mouths ever hovering but never meeting the charged, sensitive skin of the other.

At Consuelo's off-campus apartment they parted, briefly, to nod to the doorman and calmly walk up the stairs; but at the door they were at it again, each transformed into a whirl of hands and lips and tongues and desire, so single-minded in the intent to taste and touch and kiss that it took several minutes before Consuelo was able to get the key in the lock and enter the studio.

They crossed the threshold and began tearing each other's clothes off, panting now, hearts beating in their ears, and then down the fell together on the futon. Sam's mouth never left hers even as his hands eagerly explored uncharted territory, learned her dips and curves, found where he could stroke and she would groan, or gasp, or moan; or better, grab his hair and arch her body towards his, urging him on, whimpering 'please, please,' so that it was all he could do to hurriedly fumble for protection before sinking into her warmth. She bit him on the shoulder, bucking forward and pushing and meeting his thrusts, oh so deliciously, on and on until they came apart in each other's arms.

At the touch of Alessa's cold fingertips to her shoulder, Consuelo fell back to reality, acutely aware of how heavily she was breathing and how stiff her nipples were under her delicate silk dress. She finished the rest of the champagne and struggled to dive back into the conversation she left when she so conveniently had an out-of-body experience.

Benjo was gesturing to the ceiling. "…You see, we really wanted to evoke something historical and grand with The Palace, and we found this firm that specializes in this referential, old-meets-new approach to things. They showed me photos of this Duke's house in Grosvenor Square; very famous for the cutaway arches where you can observe the ballroom as you go down the stairs--"

Oh my GOD, they were still on the fucking architecture subject, Consuelo pouted.

"Oh, yes, Dorchester! How very *comme il faut*!" said Alessa.

"But really, I'm not doing it enough justice—ah, here's the man I've been looking for all night! He'll be able to explain all the details to you; he practically lives in these old places." Benjo hailed a man across the room as Alessa tittered excitedly about a small, hot design firm and the marvelous Berlin boutique hotel they did, and aren't you lucky to snag them, Benjo darling?

By now Consuelo was craning her head as well to see the mysterious wunderkind who had Alessa in such paroxysms of architectural glee. A few suits parted to let a tall, smartly dressed man pass between them.

His face moved from the shadows into the light, revealing a well-formed jaw and familiar, piercing eyes. Broad shoulders filled a navy tuxedo in a way that recalled insouciant leather jackets, and he moved with the same panther-like grace that once stalked the slick autumn streets of Chicago. Consuelo felt her heart jump in her throat and then plunge firmly all the way down to her knees.

It could not be.

"Alessa, Consuelo, please meet Sam Jose, the genius behind The Palace Hotel."

"Pleased to meet you," he said, shaking Alessa's hand, and then Consuelo's.

Their eyes met for a brief, electrically charged moment. Consuelo felt seared by the heat of his gaze, and a deep, tingling sensation traveled from where he had let his thumb stroke her palm, ever so softly and gently, deep into her heart.

It was a reminder, a confirmation: I know you, that touch said. I miss you.

"Benjo–Alessa—do you mind if I excuse myself for a moment?" said Consuelo. She turned and left, feeling Sam's gaze on her bare back the entire time. She mustered all her self-possession not to run to the ladies.' Her hands shook, her heart beat a mile a minute; the second she had the heavy brocade-paneled door to the powder room closed, she sank into the tufted chaise longue in the center of the room and dropped her head in her hands.

It could not be. It was all too much.

Sam. Her Sam. Chicago Sam. Here. Now. In her boyfriend's hotel.

It could not be.

4

Six years had passed yet the memory still stung; the pain only slightly dimmed by the passage of time.

She could not forget the look on Sam's face when he found her, finally, two hours after they had agreed to meet. Instead of at the diner he'd been boasting about to her, she was in an old gray playground on a nondescript corner in Lincoln Park. The place was tiny and sad: the ground too gravelly, the wood of the swing set and seesaw too old and warped, and the surrounding ash trees too creepy, to be of any interest to kids. Even hooligans avoided it. So she and Sam claimed it as their own: their own negative space in the world, where even the colors were inverted, and they filled it with their hushed whispers and wishes, their kisses and their love.

It was not right that they should break up here. It was not fair that she should taint their space with the problems that she thought she had escaped from Manila but had doggedly followed her here, still, across the world.

Sam sat beside her, dark eyes furious, mouth set in a straight line, and waited for her to speak. The minutes passed and their breaths fogged in the late morning air, yet the numbness of Consuelo's hands connected with the numbness of her heart, and she could not speak.

"What happened?" asked Sam, finally. "I've been calling you." He did not cajole nor did he sound all-too-ready to forgive; his tone was flat and clipped.

"I… I got a call from Ma this morning," Consuelo began. Sam looked at her from the corner of his eye, weighing each word, waiting for what came next.

"I need to go home," she finished, simply.

"Why," said Sam. He said it in the same flat, emotionless tone, so that it did not sound like a question at all, but a demand. Give me your reason. Give me a reason, and it better be good.

"They… found out about us," she said.

"So you said," he raised an eyebrow. "Last week. Why are we still talking about this? It's been a year; we practically live together. Who cares if your best friend ratted you out?" He shook his head and muttered, "At least someone had the balls to say it."

She bit her lip. "It wasn't the best…I wouldn't have--"

"If you had your way they still wouldn't know."

"That's not true, Sam."

He scoffed. "Could have fooled me."

She chose to ignore that. "It's just not the best way for them to find out, you know? Chicago was a hard sell already, and then to find out from Cora that I thought I was pregnant–I mean, what parent would want that?"

"But you're not!" he said, kicking at a pebble. "And I told you not to panic, that it's probably a false alarm, but of course you had to freak out at Cora, so–-you know what? You already know this. I already know this. What I want to know is why this is relevant to you disappearing on me this morning and threatening to go home!"

"It's not a threat, Sam; I have to go home."

"I don't think so."

She was at a loss for several moments. How could she put into words the essence of that morning's conversation; how could she summarize in a few sentences the gist of what being the only child to a family clinging desperately to lost grandeur meant? When all your pride was staked on a name, and how that name still generated something—a residue of the power it once yielded, the faint echo of a glory long gone, but still there, still something, however faint, to hold on to? How could she make him understand the complex web of loyalties she lived in and the perpetual feeling of being beholden to someone else: an almost faceless power that held the purse strings and withheld it as the whim pleased, and how she had to perpetually court its favor? How could he see how impossible it was, from where she stood, to extricate herself?

"Say something," he demanded, roughness creeping into his voice. "Did they disapprove of me?" he sneered. "Should I have prepared a dowry or something?"

"That's usually the other way around—"

"Who gives a shit?"

"Sam, please," she fought to keep her voice under control and found her hands fluttering instead. "It's my grandaunt. She's paying for everything— she paid for everything, until this morning. Mom told her about us and she…she decided to cut me off. Mom said she was almost had stroke, that they had to bring her to the hospital. She was raving all about how she didn't send me to school halfway around the world just for me to throw it all away on—on—"

"On what?" His face was inches from hers. She could see the livid splotches of color high on his cheeks and the frown line that deepened between his eyes. "No. The right question is 'On who.' Did they run a search on my last name? Ask around about my bank account? Immigrant son not good enough for their precious girl, is he?"

When she did not answer he let out a low whistle "Man. Talk about discrimination. You think you'd get it from the people who don't look like you, but no. It's the ones from The Motherland you gotta watch out for."

"Don't be that way, Sam. Don't destroy this," she

whispered.

"I'm not the one who's running away!" he exploded. "So what if she cuts you off? Can't you live without the precious trust fund?"

The slap came sudden and swift, a brief, crisp, crack in the chill air. Sam held his cheek, rubbing the raised red welt where her palm connected with his face.

"Don't you fucking dare," she cried. "You don't know what you're talking about. You don't even understand!"

"Fuck yeah, I don't understand," he said. Something seemed to be unraveling in him now, and Consuelo felt herself being taken down along with it. "I've worked every damned day of my life and—and I don't care! My family, we clawed for everything we got, but we jumped and we bet and we put our necks out and we don't care if we get our asses kicked. We fail? Well shit, at least we tried. You? You get a fucking phone call, some vague threat from your mom, and, and what? You fucking run back with your tail between your legs."

"I can't see any other choice but go back."

He shook his head. "You're legally an adult, Sue. There are other things you can do."

"Like what? Be a waitress?" she snapped.

He threw up his hands. "Oh-ho! Why not? Is that so terrible?"

"Oh, Sam."

"Don't shake your head like that, I'm serious!"

"I'm not going to fucking wait tables, all right?!"

They sat in silence for several long moments, not looking at each other. Then she laid a trembling hand on his shoulder. "I'm sorry, Sam. I just—I just feel like—like I'm out of options."

"I can think of many you haven't even thought of."

"Then tell me!" she exploded. "What do you want me to do, Sam? What do you in all your great wisdom suggest?" She tried to sneer too, but faltered. Her sarcasm failed as the naked plea came through for what it was.

"Fight," he said, evenly, with perfect clarity piercing through her confusion. "Fight for yourself. Fight for us. I don't know. Just don't calmly accept whatever it is they tell you to do. It's your life, Sue; don't let them live it for you."

A tear welled and fell down her cheek. She roughly wiped it away. "What makes you think I'm calm?"

"You seem pretty fine to me," he said, icily, to the gray winter sky.

It was too much. It felt like her heart was being ripped apart. The last year with Sam was wonderful; a respite from what she had known all her life—the careful conditioning and preparation, the endless indoctrination on family history, the feeling that she was on a collision course with a destiny already picked out for her. For the first time, she felt the possibility of a life all her own, lived away from obligations and expectations, free to choose where to go and how to live and who to love.

She should have known it was too good to be true, should have believed that those twelve months were just an illusion that could not last. She should have memorized her father's favorite maxim when she was being truculent: "At the end of the day, no one's life is truly their own."

Sam didn't understand that yet. He thought he was the captain of his own ship. It was just that there were people like her who were more aware of all the ties that bound.

So she turned and walked away from Sam without another word: deaf to his calls and pleas, unfeeling to his embraces, numb to his tears; a moving statue that plodded remorselessly until he gave up at the door of her apartment building and left her, finally, to collapse on the floor and shed all the tears that threatened to engulf them.

Within a week she was on a flight back to Manila.

The first thing she was made to do, after the car ride home filled with the endless bellowing of her father, was to throw away the phone filled with the missed calls and texts from Sam, delete her email address and deactivate her social media accounts while her mother watched and made sure that she was committing back to the cause.

After that? A useless college degree, earned from a school so low-rate she might as well not have bothered. Jobs that felt distinctly beneath her, such as the two-week sales job with the sarcastic supervisor and sexually forward clients. Well-married friends who looked at her with pity as they sipped their cocktails; indiscreetly asking if the trust fund ran out before none-too-subtly offering to set her up with Dear Hubby's Very Rich Friend.

And more of the same; grinding, depressing and cyclical; the same people, the same circles, the same advice, over the years, so much so that Consuelo realized that she had been bred to do one thing, and one thing only, and that was to be some big shot's wife. What was the use of fighting one's conditioning? So she started saying yes to the blind dates, and took the incredibly stultifying Girl Friday 'job' to one of her mom's decrepit *amigas*.

Over time, Chicago faded, becoming almost like a dream, or a favorite sequence from a fondly remembered movie. Her real dreams, of Sam holding her, kissing her, those took a while to stop invading her slumber, but soon, they did, too. She made tentative peace with her upbringing. She tried to accept her destiny. And when Benjo came into the picture, she felt ready to play the role expected of her. The past two years with him were boring and predictable and, sometimes, when she was mentally slipping up, vaguely disappointing, but at least Consuelo was on an even keel. Nothing was rocking her boat now.

Nothing, that is, until this night.

5

She touched her cheeks with cold fingertips, intently studying her face on the pin-lit vanity mirror. "Get it together, Consuelo," she said to her reflection

The distant *thunk* of a stall door told her that she was not alone, and in a few moments her reflection was joined by that of Xandra Tuason, sniffing habitually and rubbing her nose. Xandra had been three years ahead of her at her all-girls high school and was, for a brief period in her early '20s, a successful commercial model. She eventually married a congressman.

"Con," she greeted. They touched cheeks. "Staid gig, huh. Your boyfriend runs with an old crowd." Consuelo shrugged. "Then again," Xandra raised an eyebrow, "old-money approval." Her model-perfect face sneered prettily.

"Not your thing, Xandra?" she sneered back.

"I'm used to a livelier scene," she said, rubbing her nose again. "You're the only girl here I'd talk to, for, you know? Fun? I mean, God, what am I gonna say to fucking Chat Sabio, right?"

Consuelo rolled her eyes. "Yes, well. It wasn't what I expected."

"Yeah?"

"He told me it would be an intimate party."

Xandra laughed. "That's rich." She leaned closer to the mirror, scrutinizing Consuelo's face. "What's the matter, Con? You look like you've seen a ghost."

Consuelo stood up. "In a manner of speaking."

"Hey, where'ya going?"

"I need a drink."

"Cool. They have Glenmorangie. Anton's been swigging since we got here."

"You coming?"

"Nah, watching my calories." She grinned, touching the side of her nose. "I'm good."

Consuelo slunk out the powder room and went straight to the bar, giving the bartender Xandra's recommendation. She wasn't a whiskey drinker but it seemed like a good choice: something strong and dark, the definition of a stiff drink. She sipped and let the smoky, forceful taste of it fill her mouth and burn away her memories and nerves. The polished mahogany bar was solid and slick to the touch; she turned and leaned against it.

"Whiskey, eh?" said a deep voice to her side. "I'll have the same, Joc."

She braced herself with a steadying breath, turned and smiled. "Sam."

"Sue," he said, casually, not realizing the gut-punch effect the old pet name had on Consuelo, who sipped whiskey to hide the wince on her face.

"Trust Sam Jose to know the bartender's name before The Palace even opens."

He pulled her hand delicately and leaned to sniff her tumbler. "Fancy. I remember you being partial to boxed wine."

"Says the guy who introduced me to them." She rubbed the shiny lapel of his tuxedo. "Now this is fancy."

There was so much about him that was familiar—the sardonic smile, the way his upper lip quirked before he teased her, the intent way he looked at her and that made her feel like she was being read, like an open book. Yet there was much that was changed, too. Up close she noticed the subtlety of his obviously expensive haircut. There was discernible tension in the way he held his jaw, which contrasted with the suave, louche way he sat and played with his suit buttons and the studied elegance in the way he held his own drink. There was something wary and guarded in the brown eyes that were once so open and guileless.

"So fancy no one will guess I'm basically here to collect my payment?"

She laughed—it wasn't that it was funny; it was just that there was a palpable, thick silence between them and she had to fill it, somehow.

"I mean it. I have a meeting in Hong Kong tomorrow night, but someone held my check hostage until he was sure I'd come." He rolled his eyes and tapped his suit. "Just now I checked and it's finally deposited. The bastard. He knows I fucking can't stand these big hoorays." He seemed so annoyed it was easy to forget how he spiffed up for the big hooray in what looked like a custom Paul Smith.

"So what's your story, Sue?" he asked casually, sipping his drink.

"Oh, you know. Same old, same old," she followed his lead.

"Cut the shit," he said, smiling affably but with real acid in his tone. Suddenly the playful banter turned dark. "So this is the elusive Consuelo De la Red in her native habitat." He started a Brit accent, an attempt at a Richard Attenborough impression. "The milieu smells of money. Society types abound. The air crackles with fake cheer. The explorer watches cautiously, wary of being eaten."

She pursed her lips and put on her haughtiest expression. "Don't be a dick, Sam."

He chuckled without humor. "Too late for that."

"Besides, you're not the outsider anymore, Mr.

Explorer," she said. "'Oh, look at these historic London manor details and my hot architectural career in Europe,' whatever."

Something shifted in his gaze: some of the wariness slipped, and he bit his lip. "I clean up good, don't I?"

Sam took a moment to steady himself as she uncrossed her hands and let the psychic ice thaw between them.

His mind flew back to the day they had first met, in line for hotdogs a long time ago. She had been surprised when he told her he knew she wasn't a regular. In his mind he thought: Because if you were, I would have noticed you before. He remembered admiring her well-shaped legs in tight jeans, the curve of her bottom peeking from a short leather coat, and the first thrill of seeing her face: sleepy bedroom eyes, lush red lips, a shock of tousled dark hair under a gray knit beret. It was a face made for watching, and in their year together he did watch it, warily, as a sailor on the lookout for storms on the horizon would, but also for the rays of sunshine that more often than not greeted his mornings.

Her hauteur was replaced by a soft smile, "So what have you been up to?" She looked up and around her, her gaze sweeping over the cutaway arches that had so besotted Alessa, down to the graceful, curving bar top underneath her hands. "I mean, all of this? What happened to taking over your dad's business?"

"It is my dad's business."

"Funny, I don't remember you mentioning your dad heading an avant garde architecture firm big in Europe."

He shook his head. "Dad was an architect. Before we migrated. Construction was just the more logical choice over in Chicago."

"Still, there's a pretty huge gap between local construction business to posh international practice. How did that happen?"

He waved his drink in a gesture that toasted her while

dismissing the question. "A lot can happen in six years."

"Too true. Six years is a long time."

He sipped his drink again, his gaze softening as he stared at her. He leaned close. Softly, tentatively, moved a forefinger from her wrist up to her elbow. "Six years," he murmured, softly caressing her skin, waiting for her to draw back and suppressing an inner smile when she stayed where she was, welcoming his touch. "So many things change, but there are some things that stay the same."

She suppressed a gasp as his feather-light stroke raised goosebumps up her arm.

He bent closer to whisper, "You're still beautiful, Sue."

Her heart started beating madly against her ribs; she was sure he could hear it. She shakily sipped her drink to place some distance between them.

A bell rang and uniformed waiters began circulating amongst them, collecting glasses and announcing dinner.

The guests rose and filed into the other end of the ballroom, cleverly partitioned with painted screens and rare plants. Consuelo took advantage of the din of activity to pull away from Sam. She could make out Benjo just ahead of her, intently listening to someone who seemed to be the chairman of the country's top rated TV network.

Xandra fell into step and linked arms with her. "Oooh," purred Xandra, as they stepped through the screens. Instead of the expected litter of round, numbered tables, there was a vast, L-shaped table, long enough to seat all the guests, with waiters dressed as footmen standing at intervals between the chairs.

"Where the heck are we sitting?" slurred Congressman Anton Tuason, Xandra's husband.

Benjo stopped and waited for Consuelo at the head of the line as the maître d'hotel (in coattails, of course) showed him the seating chart.

Xandra let out a low, flirtatious whistle. "Your

boyfriend, huh," she whispered to Consuelo. "Footmen, precedence and butlers?"

Consuelo didn't wait to catch Xandra's punchline and left to take her place by Benjo's side. "Where were you earlier?" he asked, discreetly shooting a look at the TV network bigwig. "You missed Abdon Delgado. He was… better than I expected. Anyway. No matter. I still think he was impressed." He gave a signal, and the footmen, headed by the maître d' hotel, began seating the guests.

Consuelo was led away from Benjo—of course, she realized; Benjo really wanted to old-school-tradition this all the way. Couples separated, new connections encouraged at the table. Careful thought was put into who would sit beside whom. A sense of precedence pervaded, as if this were a matter of aristocracy than oligarchy. The more important and influential people got the prime seats along the vast table, becoming the centers of little clustered islands of attention, while the more jocular guests—particularly the pretty wives and girlfriends—liberally sprinkled to lubricate the conversation.

She was seated beside Congressman Tuason, farther from Benjo than she expected. Wondering what Benjo wanted from the Congressman, she started reviewing how he'd mentioned the politician so that she could steer their conversation accordingly. Her boyfriend ceded the position of honor at the end of the table to his father, sitting on the elder's right, while a giggling, forearm-stroking Alessa Bruckner-Jones was deposited opposite them.

Consuelo scanned the table for Xandra and found her gabbing animatedly to Chairman Abner Delgado, leaving a bored-looking Chat Sabio to gaze in the distance. A footman showed a guest to her right and, of course, because it was this kind of night, Sam Jose sat next to her.

"So. We meet again." He looked amused.

"Funny. We seem to keep doing that today."

Linen napkins were unfolded on their laps, orders for

the mains quietly taken from them by handsomely efficient waiters. They sunk into twinkling, inconsequential small talk with their seatmates. Between Consuelo and Sam, however, lay an electrically charged silence.

The first course arrived, a tiny amuse bouche consumed in a few hesitant bites, and then came the second, some sort of fish wrapped in origami-like pastry. Wines were refilled and Sam took advantage of the susurrus of excited conversation to whisper:

"I don't know about you but I could go for a hot dog right now."

A nostalgic smile spread on Consuelo's face. "I would, too," she agreed.

"Kinda hard to do that with what you're wearing," he said, his gaze slipping down her décolletage.

"You're not dressed for fast food, either," she said, trying to keep the conversation businesslike.

"You wouldn't last two seconds in a Hot Doug's line with your back out like that."

She turned to him. "My dress making you uncomfortable, Sam?"

He took in the sight of her like a parched man savoring a long drink of water. "Completely the opposite, Sue. I am so comfortable right now."

His gaze was forthright and direct, cool on the surface, but Consuelo heated under his eyes. The thing about him that drove her crazy was that he could shoot her a look where she read all the naughty things he wanted to do to her, and yet, to anyone else outside their almost telepathic connection, he was simply looking. That this connection, long dead, should be resurrected so quickly over dinner despite six years apart, flustered her.

"Tell me something," he murmured, catching a flap of fabric from her skirt and playing with it between his fingers. She glanced at his hand, deftly stroking the silk in a slow, round, languorous motion, and remembered all those nights when his fingers were in her; she felt her center clench deliciously.

"Hmm?" she mumbled, a little breathless.

"So. You and Benjo."

The fork traveled to her mouth almost beyond her volition. She chewed mindlessly, not tasting the food.

"That's the guy you're with," he continued. She raised an eyebrow in assent. "Benjo is the kind of guy your family wants you to be with." He stated this matter of fact; but it made Consuelo feel small and harshly judged.

"Yes, Sam," she smiled sweetly, a contrast to the archness of her tone.

He withdrew his hand and shrugged. "That guy. Really. Approval all the way?"

She wouldn't look at him, but her face was the picture of irritated bitchery. "Yes."

"And he has their blessing, so you just, I dunno, went with it?"

"Mm-hmm."

"Must be great to have someone else make up your mind for you, no?"

"Yes and yes to the Spanish Inquisition," she snapped. She spread her hands on her lap and began whispering to the wineglass.

"Anything else you want to know? Maybe how we were set up on a date by my grandaunt and how the whole clan harangued me for weeks to go out with him? How we had geoduck for our first dinner even if I can't stand the stuff because it's his favorite and I couldn't even tell him where I wanted to go? And that his mother was there? And we didn't have anything to talk about, except my uncles? Or how my mom, like, shrieked in happiness because his family sent over a gift box the day after our date? It was a box of tea. Fucking *expensive* tea, but still. Tea. And how, the way she went on about it, this wooden box of dried leaves was proof that this guy I barely knew was The One."

The waiters replaced their plates with a delicate cup of

palate-cleansing sorbet. Consuelo took a heaping teaspoon and let the cool, tangy, slightly bitter taste of it coat her tongue.

Sam left his untouched. After a minute, he said, "You know he likes to whore around, don't you?"

A tremor in her teaspoon-clutching hand was all the indication that she'd heard him.

"We'd done business meetings here, in Hong Kong, even once in Amsterdam," he continued, watching her spoon the icy slush into her mouth. "Every single night, that's what he wanted to do. Visit a whorehouse— the sleazier, the better. Always brought a girl home. Or two."

She set the spoon down as though it weighed a ton.

"Let me guess." Her knuckles were white on the silverware. "You were the only pure, saintly one who didn't buy pussy."

The way she hesitated before she said 'pussy' reminded him of all the times he teased her for her inability to say crude things with the requisite gravitas, and he suppressed a tiny ache in his heart. Swirling the sorbet in the cup, he mused, "One of these days he's going to give you a disease, you know."

"Wouldn't you like that?" she asked lightly.

He caught her hand and brought it under the table. "No," he said, putting as much force as he could into the syllable. "To see you suffer—to see you get hurt—that's the last thing I want."

Her face was a mask, carefully studied and smoothed so that only the movement of her lips and her quivering pulse betrayed the life in her. "Funny. I wouldn't have guessed that, with what you've been saying to me since we saw each other."

His grip tightened. "So you do feel, after all."

"I'm not made of stone."

"You had me fooled."

She yanked her hand from his grasp and finally faced

him. "What is it that you want, Sam?"

"You," he said quickly, his eyes smoldering and locking deep into hers, his body tense and coiled, ready to fight. "It's always been you."

Consuelo looked away first and silently prayed to the culinary gods for their mains to arrive. "Don't do this, Sam. Not now."

"When is it ever a good time?" he countered. "Hell, you walked out of my life six years ago, no word no nothing, and I couldn't find you or speak to you or get in touch, or beg—and I wanted to do that, all of that. Tonight I find out that the asshole I do business with gets to call *my* girl 'his,' and fuck if I'm not going to do anything about it. I was ready to beg for you, Sue, and I will."

The mains finally arrived, but Consuelo stared through the plate of sea bass with almond truffle risotto.

Consuelo was a master of concealment, but all throughout the year they spent together, Sam had learned how to peek behind the veil. Tonight he wondered if the skill deserted him; if her reaction to his touch and his words were assigned a meaning that was only true in his mind. But seeing her now, fighting for control, confirmed his wishes and gave him hope as he had never hoped before.

He caught her hand and brought it under the table again; he caressed her wrist and let his fingers trail over her pulse, working into her clenched fist until the tremor subsided and her palm opened, accepting his touch.

"Look at me," he whispered, leaning closer now. "Look at me now and tell me you're happy with Benjo. That you're happy hanging off his arm, like an accessory, while he grab-hands some rich fucker." Tugging her hand slightly, he continued: "If this is the life you want, just say the word and I'll shut up. I'll shut up and collect the balance he owes me and then I'll get on that plane tomorrow, and that's the last you'll ever hear or see of me."

Her eyes gazed out at him through a curtain of wet lashes.

"Just say the word," he said.

She parted her mouth to speak.

The words were there, a speech rehearsed, standing on the tip of Consuelo's tongue. The words were what was expected of her: all her life, all her training, everyone who had been approved and allowed into her sphere, the schools she was put into, the conversations she'd heard and the values drilled into her head: The doctrine of the Family Name. The alliance they'd all sought. Make Benjo happy. Be the cherry on top of his career triumph sundae. Get the diamond ring and finally seal the deal. It was all here, right now, at this table. All that stood between the culmination of everyone's plan for her was the man holding her hand under the table.

Sam's face was earnest, expectant. All she had to do was say the words, and this obstacle, too, would be destroyed.

She found her voice.

"It's too late, Sam."

She turned and started a conversation with Congressman Tuason, the picture of the well-bred lady helping her boyfriend get ahead in his career by charming his network. No one could have guessed that she felt like she was crumbling inside, and it took all of her willpower not to let it show.

6

The green silk train swished softly over the thick carpet as Consuelo paced in the hallway fronting her room. She breathed hard, fighting harder to calm herself, but her frantic state of mind manifested through her hands, flapping and fluttering to her neck; dropping to her belly; flying this way and that

This was it. She had made her choice. She had broken Sam's heart again, perhaps forever. Benjo and the life laid out for her—it was the path she chose. There was no turning back.

Yet despite her conviction when the said the words, the dinner had remained an ordeal for her. She built an invisible wall so that she could not see Sam as she charmed Congressman Tuason. But the mounting panic soon overwhelmed her, and when the meal ended she rushed to Benjo to let him know she was going to freshen up—but all she got was a scolding in return. ("You interrupted the Chairman to tell me that? Well go on then.") But just as she reached her door she realized she'd left her clutch—and key card—in her dining seat. Now she was locked out, and agitated, and feeling worse than before.

Footsteps, muffled on the thick carpet but still making

an impression on her heightened nerves, made her jump and shrink against the wall. Her heart kicked in her chest as the approaching figure resolved into focus.

"Go away, Sam," her voice shook. "Please. Just go."

He approached, still, his face grim but determined, holding her clutch in one hand. "I thought you might want this."

Frozen to her post, she nodded, incapable of moving an inch. If she came to him, if she touched him, her mask would shatter, her resolve would crumble, and it could all come crashing down.

"Aren't you going to get it?" He drew closer and reached out to her. She took a tentative step and snatched it from his grasp. A flash of hurt passed in his eyes, and he covered it with a quick, easy laugh. "Am I that gross? Won't you even touch my hand?"

The laugh could not disguise the naked plea underneath his flippant tone. She could not bear his expression crumbling before her, and she shut her eyes against the sight.

His hand sought hers, followed by the other. The clutch fell to the floor, and her breath rushed out of her in a sob.

"Look at me," pleaded Sam. "For God's sake. The least you can do is open your eyes and tell me, straight to my face, that you choose him." He grasped her chin. "Look at me!"

"I—I choose him," she quavered, eyes still shut tight.

"Liar," Sam whispered. "Look me in the eye when you say it."

Forcing her eyes to open, she parted her lips to speak, but before the words could come out Sam kissed her—roughly, firmly; his mouth demanding the choice her words could not make.

Such was the volatility of her emotions, the precarious balance of the war in her heart, that the second his lips met hers her body betrayed the resolution of her mind.

She met his kiss avidly, hungrily; she threaded her hands in his hair and clung to him, afraid that they would part.

Groaning, his hands grasped her waist and pulled her body against his. Everywhere their skin met felt like fire. The kiss deepened into something that skirted the edge of savagery; their tongues warred and tasted each other, relearning once-intimate geography. She moaned into his mouth and it was all that he could do not to lose control. He drove against the wall to steady himself, pinning her body against his. Her legs parted for him, and he relished the gasp that broke from her as she felt his hardness against her core. He took advantage of her surprise to move his lips against her neck.

"Sam…Sam…" his name filled her mind and tumbled out her mouth. His hands moved from her waist to her ribcage, hovering, maddeningly, right underneath the swell of her breasts. A thumb moved slowly to stroke that space where the skin began to full, driving her to arch her back and cling to him tighter.

His mouth moved hungrily across her collarbone and down the strip skin beneath exposed by her dress. She whimpered now as his tongue tasted the space above her heart. "Gorgeous, I know," he murmured, desire rising like a wave inside of him as he felt her heartbeat quicken under his lips. His hands traveled up and down her sides as his mouth followed the cut of her dress.

He moved back to her mouth and kissed her again, slow this time, savoring instead of devouring. His lips moved to the sensitive place beneath her ear to whisper, "Did you miss me?"

"Yes." Her voice was barely a breath, the single syllable containing a wealth of desire, and she arched against him once again.

"Baby, I miss you too," he groaned, sliding a hand

underneath her bodice. Her gasp urged him on, but he let his fingers hover first, teasing her, and he let his other hand idly trace heated patterns on her bare back.

Frustrated, she grabbed a fistful of his hair and bit his lip. He laughed now and gave in: his thumb stroked her breast, relearning the bounty of it flush against his touch; he ran the thumb over the hard peak of her nipple and laughed again when she drew her head back and moaned.

"No one makes you feel like I did, do they?" he murmured, and now his mouth was on hers again, swallowing her answer. She quivered in his arms and slid her arm down his chest, down to his waist. The ghostly touch of her fingers against his belly made his heart jump. He pinched her nipple and she shuddered, pulling his shirt free.

"Touch me," he commanded, and her hands obeyed, trailing over his abdomen and brushing against his straining erection.

He growled and pushed the bodice to one side, exposing one white breast. His mouth was on it even as she begged him to "Kiss me, please," swirling his tongue over her nipple. With a strangled cry she moved to meet his hardness, moving to ease the ache in her core, but before she could do it again he grasped her hips, hands restlessly hovering over her skirt, his mouth working feverishly on her until he found the slit in front of her dress. His hand traveled from hip to slit and up the creamy expanse of her thighs until it found the damp seam of her thong.

"Sam…" she sighed, and the hopeless surrender of it almost undid him. He slipped a finger under the fabric to stroke her inner lips. Her breathing hitched and her hips ground against the wall, so he dipped his finger inside to touch her moist center.

"Sam!" she said again, breathless and excited, and he played inside her, moving his mouth over hers so that he could kiss every moan and grasp that tumbled out of her lips.

"Baby, I don't care," he said, suddenly and savagely, as she broke their kiss to lick a trail down his neck. "I don't care if you choose him." His other hand tightened, almost painfully, against her hip. "If all we have is this night, and only this night, I'll take it."

"Sam—"

"I'll take it," he repeated, angry now. "Just be mine tonight."

She took his face in her hands and looked into his fever-bright eyes. Both their mouths were puffy with kisses; four sets of pupils were dilated with arousal. But he knew that in his eyes there was something else altogether: a desperate resignation that he hoped she could see and strike her deep in her soul.

She was about to say something when, from a distance, the chimes of a bell cut through the fog of desire enveloping them.

"The ball is starting," she said, hurriedly pulling back and fixing her dress. "Some of them will be changing for the dance," she explained, but Sam had already bent to hand her clutch, then straightened to tuck his shirt and button up his suit.

"Go inside and fix your make up," he said as she fumbled for the card key. Before she could get the door closed, however, he caught her arm. "This isn't over, Sue," he said. He released her just as the voices of the changing guests echoed down the hall.

She shut the door and slumped against it, trying to master her racing heart. Pressed her ear against the wood she could make out Sam greeting another guest and exchanging a few snippets of small talk. After a while silence descended on the floor. Consuelo sat in front of the vanity mirror and began to reapply her make up with shaking hands.

7

"How are you feeling?" said Benjo, appraising her from head to foot. He touched the back of his hand to her pale forehead. "You're clammy. Something you ate?"

They stood at the edge of the shiny hardwood dance floor with the rest of the guests. The jazz singer moved through the lyrics of *Perhaps, Perhaps, Perhaps*, her voice sinuous as the slithering of a snake and soft enough for them to carry on a refined conversation.

"Just tired," she mumbled.

Benjo grunted and turned to watch the appreciative crowd. "You need to manage that, Con," he scolded. "You've been disappearing on me all night, just when I need you. That's not what I want."

"Sorry, Benjo." She managed to keep her expression placid even as a twinge of irritation seized her.

The applause and flourish as the song ended drowned out his reply, whatever it was. The band struck up a bass heavy, dance-y tune, and couples began to fill the dance floor to do their carefully practiced ballroom routines. Middle-aged partners in sequins and couture jigged and Charleston'd and swung to the singer's deep and expressive voice.

Benjo clapped along, tapped his foot and did that long-distance crowd conversation thing where one points, smiles and mouths encouragement to anyone who happens to meet one's eye.

Xandra was doing a borderline lascivious lambada with the TV Chairman. Chat Sabio, with Consuelo's father Rudy, managed to dance without actually moving outside an imaginary one-by-one foot square on the floor. Concha laughed and whispered to Benjo's dad as they did a gentle swing. The song segued into a jazzed-up pop standard, and more people stood from their seats and joined the bodies on the dance floor.

Alessa walked across the dance floor straight to them, curvaceous hips swinging generously under her black gown, the spangles of her dress catching the light. Consuelo had to give it to her: the woman knew how to make an entrance.

"My dear Benjo! *What* are you doing here, at the edge of the party?" she demanded, eyes wide, as though Benjo not dancing was a Matter of Life and Death.

He laughed sheepishly. "Ah, I couldn't, Alessa. Don't want to embarrass myself."

"Oh, but that's not what I heard!" she trilled.

"Besides," he continued, "Consuelo's not feeling well. Got to keep her company."

"Nonsense!" she laughed. "Consuelo darling." She grasped her forearms. "You're not one of these absurd women who simply cannot exist at a party without their Significant Other by their sides at all times, are you?"

"Far from it," said Consuelo, showing all her teeth.

"There!" said Alessa triumphantly. "Consuelo doesn't mind; what do you say to a little dance?" She wiggled her hip against him and raised her hands as she said this.

"Well, if it's OK—" he said, turning up the self-deprecation act.

"Shoo," said Consuelo, waving her hands. "It's fine. Go on!"

Alessa led him into the middle of the crowd and began to insinuate herself against him in little undulating movements, graceful but unmistakably sexy. Consuelo, watching half-heartedly, remembered Alessa's stint as a belly dancing instructor to the elite during the wilderness years (pre-Bruckner-Jones) and mentally commended her for keeping lithe.

A waiter approached with her order of Long Island Iced Tea. She drank it slowly, mindful that she had barely eaten and eager to avoid any more compromising situations. She squirmed in her seat, heat rising to her cheeks when she remembered the events of the previous hour. How could she lose control like that, in front of her room, in an open hallway? She would get into trouble and nothing would be good.

And yet.

And yet, when she left her suite to return to the ball, the first thing she did was scan the sea of people for Sam's face. When their eyes briefly met from across the room, she felt her knees go weak and her heart turn to jelly. Would it be worth it to be in trouble for him? She mentally replayed everything that Sam had said:

You. It's always been you.
I was ready to beg for you, Sue, and I will.
If all we have is this night, and only this night, I'll take it.

Her thoughts were a jumbled, tangled mess. Before this night she thought she had made peace with her fate. She would do what was expected of her, and make everyone happy, for a change. She would not disappoint them anymore. She would no longer read the bitterness in the eyes of her parents and relatives: There she is, the selfish one, the one without any sense of devotion to the family that strove to give her everything. The wanderlust in her veins, the rebelliousness of her nature—she'd gotten them out of her system, finally. She was in her mid-twenties now; a perfectly acceptable time to settle down and let the demons of her past go.

But Sam's reappearance, on this night of all nights, threw all of those resolutions into a jumble. How he touched her, how he kissed her—it was true what he said; no one had ever made her feel that way before, or since.

Other questions arose in her head, questions she considered long buried. True, Benjo would take care of her—financially, if not in any other aspect. "All you need," said her father, "is someone who knows his duty, and abides by it. To expect anything more is foolishness."

But did she not deserve love? Did she not deserve devotion? Was she not worthy of someone who thought of her through the years, and carried a torch for her, and felt as strongly for her as if those intervening years never happened?

Was she not worthy of someone for whom she felt as strongly, despite the passage of time?

"Penny for your thoughts," slurred a voice, slick as gasoline, in her ear.

"Xandra." Her friend dropped in the seat beside her, daintily dabbing away at the sweat on her temples. Her pupils were dilated and she had a jittery, flushed look to her. "You all right?"

"Yeah-yeah," smiled Xandra, bright as a new coin.

"Where's Anton?"

She waved her hands in the air. "Probably at the bar. Glenmorangie is his *faaaavorite*," she giggled. "Why aren't you dancing? Boy, what a cut-up! That Chairman something is grabby-grabby. Like fending off an octopus, geez! I had to excuse myself; I was starting to feel like a stress ball." Xandra signaled the waiter for water, chugged it down, and then motioned with fluttering fingers to the dance floor.

"Why's that bitch Alessa Bruckner-Jones grinding against your man?" she continued, soon as she drew breath.

Consuelo followed the tilt of her chin to see Alessa still doing her undulating dance move, but this time with her back to Benjo. He had both hands on her hips now, and she could make out how he would flex them against her as though controlling himself from pulling her ass against him. She threw him coy little over-the-shoulder looks, egging him on.

"They wanted to dance?" Consuelo shrugged, perfectly above it all.

"I don't trust that *noblewoman*." Xandra put the last words in air quotes. "She was talking shit about you in the bathroom, you know."

"I don't care." It was true. It was amazing how much she did not care, Consuelo found.

If Xandra heard anything she didn't give any indication—she had a juicy story to spill and her audience's indifference was no deterrent. "You should have heard the bitch, Con. She was going on and on about how Benjo had his grandma's diamond ring reset and how *spectaaaacular* it was, and what a shame it would be that it was only going to you."

Consuelo felt punched in the gut. All night long the fact of Benjo's looming 'surprise' would pop up and jar her, but she was unwilling to truly think it through. Like any good compartmentalizer she shoved it into the "Deal With Later" file in her head and went about her business.

But Xandra's gossip had a way of dusting off the file and making that abstract bit of unpleasantness a very real thing shoved in her face. What would she do when the moment came and the ring was presented to her? A week ago it had been clear; but like someone who'd been talked into a bungee jump she stood right at the precipice and the survivalist in her head started to talk her off the ledge.

"…yeah, what a backbiter! Ugh, Con, if I only didn't want to make a scene, I would've yanked her dress and shoved those silicon boobs up her face, the hag," Xandra continued, her happy, hyper demeanor an interesting contrast to her words.

The band ended with a flourish. Alessa parted from Benjo by kissing him on both cheeks, whispering a bit in his ear, and dragging her hand against his. He took the seat opposite Consuelo and nodded at her drink. "Feeling better now, honey?" The sarcasm dripped from his tone.

"Much, thanks."

On stage the band retreated to let the evening's host, one of Benjo's flunkies, call on Benjo's father for his remarks.

Polite applause filled the room as the elder Yu shambled up the stage. His bald pate gleamed in the spotlight, and people tried not to remark too much on the shininess of his vest or how dreadfully gauche his snakeskin shoes were.

But people could not help tuning out Mr. Yu's long and rambling speech. He even had a slide show projected behind him and went through the highlights, chronologically, of his beloved son's life.

"His aptitude for business was very much in evidence," Mr. Yu monotoned, "when he topped his year, every year, for the most number of bingo tickets sold at his school's Foundation Day fundraising drive. That was when Lita and I knew: we have raised a real Yu."

There was a smattering of laughter at this. Benjo went along appreciatively but had started to jiggle his leg and fidget in his seat. In contrast, Consuelo retreated into herself, clamping down on her twitching hands and striving to master her panic. Every second longer Mr. Yu droned was a second delaying Benjo's grand finale to the evening.

Mr. Yu took them from high school into Benjo's successful scholarship application to business school abroad and apprenticeship at a property developer in Hong Kong.

"And so it is with the utmost pride that I congratulate my only son, Benjamin Einstein Yu, on the inauguration of

The Palace Hotel," Mr. Yu croaked. "It will be the jewel in the All-Star Property Corp. crown and a glittering scepter in the skyline of Manila. Son, you have proven yourself to me and your mother. I do not often say this, but I look around me, and see all the new friends we have made tonight, and all I have to say is: Son. You were right."

He looked straight at Benjo as he said this. Applause exploded around them, but between father and son there seemed to be a symbolic exchange going on—an understanding reached, a torch passed. Benjo smiled tightly and went up to hug his father. It was a stiff, awkward embrace, but a sign of affection nevertheless. They patted each other's backs with as minimal contact as possible, and went his own way: Mr. Yu back to his seat, Benjo to the mic.

Consuelo's stomach turned somersaults and leapt through flaming rings. Onstage, her boyfriend was magnetic. Handsome and affable, a counterpoint to the stiff man who sired him, he cracked a few jokes and got the crowd relaxed. When she looked at him like this, from afar, she could almost believe that she could share a life with him. If he could favor her with a small percentage of the effort and energy he spent charming strangers, perhaps being married to him would not be such a scary prospect—blue collar sex habit notwithstanding. As he stood onstage, in his element, at a distance from Consuelo, she mused that she could possibly even be happy with him.

It was what would happen when the spotlight was off and the distance between them erased that cast a dark cloud over her hopes.

"…There are so many people that are responsible for The Palace Hotel." He smiled winningly. "Some of them designed it, some of them built it, some of them did the unglamorous job of shepherding it through paperwork and government approvals. Some of them are even here, this night, at this gathering of close friends" (to Consuelo's left,

Xandra sputtered to hold in a guffaw) "and I believe they deserve every bit of applause this evening."

The crowd obliged, giving these nameless someones a standing ovation.

Benjo continued.

"I'd also like to call up to the stage my beautiful Consuelo—"

THUD THUD THUD went her heartbeat, hammering against the door of her chest like a prisoner dying to escape.

"— come up and join me, honey." He seemed to glow onstage, every bit a star.

On shaking legs she walked, off the chair, across the glimmering dance floor, up the stage, beside her boyfriend. Her mask was in place but it threatened to slip from the quaking of her nerves. The faces of all their 'friends' gazed up appraisingly; watching, waiting, calculating. At the front of the crowd was her father, impassive, but with approval glittering in face. Less able to control her delight was her mother, who fidgeted and grabbed Rudy's arm and smiled and tittered to her seatmates. Alessa had a huge smile on her face, eyes bright and wide with feigned delight.

Consuelo's found the one face she wanted to see. His was at the back, by the bar, far from the light cast by the stage, but still in the dimness she could see the grim expectation in his face, the set mouth, the eyes that stared back, hard and despondent.

"You know, Con and Tito Rudy and Tita Concha, they supported me when no one believed in my dream," said Benjo, taking her by the hand. "I was just a young gun with nostalgia for the past and the ambition to build a hotel that would make people remember Manila's Golden Age. A lot of people said it couldn't be done; and if it did, no one would appreciate it. But maybe because Tito Rudy and Tita Concha are of and espouse that Golden Age themselves—it flows through their veins and lives in their home—they never doubted me even for one second."

He paused to let the crowd react appropriately. Consuelo watched her mom accept pats on the back from her seatmates.

Validation looked great on her.

"And Con, my sweet girl. She is always there for me."

How generic, a snarky voice in the back of Consuelo's head cut through the panic with a sneer.

But then Benjo began to reach inside his suit.

Oh no. Oh no. OH NO NO NO NO.

All of Consuelo's alarm bells turned red and blared klaxons. Her hands began to shake, and curiously Benjo seemed to move a lot slower, like a DVD set to slow-motion. His hand worked its way in the inside pocket of his suit. The smile brightened, the eyes glanced to hers in expectation, and then the hand stopped wriggling and began to draw something out.

In her panic Consuelo scanned the crowd for a savior—some sensible person who would read her mind and would put a stop to this. Her eye jumped from person to person: her father, her mother, Alessa (smiling ever wider), Xandra (yawning), Congressman Anton (red as a beet), and finally, Sam (looking away). It was his grimace of pain, his refusal to see what was happening, that finally spurred her to move.

She reached out to push the mic away from them and leaned into Benjo's ear.

"Please. Don't," she pleaded.

"What?" He still smiled, but there was steel his voice.

"Please. Whatever this is. Whatever you're holding. Don't."

"Don't be silly, Consuelo—"

"Don't," she said, forcefully now, emotion spilling over her voice. "Please. Please listen to me. Don't. Not now."

He drew back and stared at her for a few moments. In his look she read anger and disbelief and annoyance. Consuelo stared right back and shook her head, firmly.

The grip on her hand tightened painfully and she bit back a yelp of hurt. He worked to remove the tenseness from his mouth and force it into a grin. The hand withdrew from the suit pocket, but it was, mercifully, empty.

"Ha-ha," Benjo laughed hollowly into the mic. "It seems we have a shy one here."

Consuelo pasted an answering grin on her face, knowing that she must have looked a fright: a ghastly pumpkin smile sharing space with wild-eyed panic.

Her gaze skittered over the crowd again like a rock skipping on water. It jumped over the bemused or indifferent expressions of the guests, the outrage on her mom's, the glee on Alessa's and the slightly interested one on Xandra's, to find the hope and the joy on Sam's. He leaned forward, eager, hanging on to every word issued from the stage.

She smiled her fright mask smile wider and shook her head again, this time vigorously so that even the people in the back of the room could not mistake her refusal.

Benjo bit his lip and fixed her a hard stare. "Well then," he said after a few tense moments.

Consuelo bowed her head and played the shy coquette.

"Well then," Benjo repeated, injecting his tone with forced lightness. "It's the shy ones you have to treasure, right?" The crowd cheered their assent. "Full of surprises."

Benjo wrapped up his speech with a few more platitudes and a whole lot of flattery, but Consuelo couldn't hear any of it. All that registered was the slosh of blood pounding in her ears.

She had fucked up.

Benjo fielded a group of bigwigs and well-wishers she hurried down the stage, the only thought in her head was how she had fucked up *utterly*.

The extent of her SNAFU was revealed when she descended and found herself pulled close to her parents in a parody of a family powwow. Her father leaned his face away from his disgrace of a daughter.

"What was that all about?" hissed Concha.

Consuelo's tongue was tied in knots and she could not answer.

"We'll talk about this later," she hissed again, releasing her daughter's arm with such force that it flew, almost windmilling behind her.

Consuelo rubbed her arm and stood as straight as she could to show everyone that the motion had hurt. Her mother looked stricken—she realized she just manhandled her grown daughter in front of Manila's elite, who now buzzed in hushed whispers, eyebrows raised in judgment around them. They had all seen it, and her mother knew it.

The fright in her mother's face galvanized Consuelo somehow; confirmed that she had nothing left to lose. There was nothing else to do but walk. She sailed past her parents, past Alessa (she did not even stop to acknowledge the woman's improvised bon mot), past the excited Xandra, through the crowd, and all the way to the bar at the back of the room.

Sam sat with his back to her, but she could almost sense the smile on his face. She asked the bartender for a glass of water.

"Room 3410," said Sam, so soft it was almost as if she imagined it, and then he got up, gave the bartender a tip, and left the ballroom.

When her glass was drained, she asked for a shot of bourbon. When that was gone, she got up and followed him.

8

Room 3410, when she found it, was a plain white door with curling gold letters set in a rococo frame. Consuelo stopped at this plain, unassuming door, and with trembling hands, knocked.

"It's open," Sam's voice rang from within.

Fingers cold with nerves curled on the gold door handle and pushed.

Her eyes took a moment to adjust to the dimness of the room. It was smaller than her adjoining suite, but any difference in décor and material was lost on her. All she could process was the man standing by the window with his jacket off and bowtie loose, watching the lights of Manila glint and twinkle from the 34th floor, illuminated by the warm yellow light of a single lamp by his feet.

She closed the door behind her and waited, not knowing what to do or say. It was done. She had nothing more to lose. Benjo lost face at the moment that was supposed to be his crowning glory. Her parents were livid and close to possibly disowning her. What she would do tomorrow was not clear. All that mattered was that she had come, here, now, to her old lover's room. It was as much choice as she could muster tonight. What happened next was up to him.

He turned and looked at her, finally. "So," he said. "We meet again."

"We seem to do that a lot," she answered.

"Seems so," he agreed, still smiling, maddeningly, all the way across the room from her. He tilted his head and studied her face for a very long while. Her body quivered under the intensity of his gaze. How she longed for him to come to her, to touch her, to give her the comfort she sought from this long, strange night.

"Let's pretend," he finally said. "Or do things over. Press reset and go back to the beginning." He ran his hands through his hair in frustration. "Whatever—I'm not making sense tonight." His expression cleared and took on some of its old openness. "Hi. I'm Sam," he said affably.

She played along. "Consuelo."

"Cawn-sway-low," he repeated.

She had to laugh at that, and the sudden mirth helped release the tension holding her spine straight and tight. She sank to the bed and cradled her forehead in her hands. "You're butchering it," she said softly.

"Maybe I'll just call you Sue," he said.

"You're the only one who does."

Something tugged at his heart at her words, bringing back the memories of their time together, all the small moments, pet names and private jokes that made up the secret language that they, like all lovers, devised; a dialect that died when they broke up. But now it came back to him, a language rising from memory and falling easily from his tongue. "So what's your story, Sue?"

She ran her hand across her face and sighed. "How much time you got, Sam?"

"All night long, Gorgeous."

She smiled again, but it was fleeting and faint, and she still had her hand across her eyes. "I fucked up, Sam. Utterly fucked things up. I was at the very moment where everyone's plans for me would finally, finally come true, and what did I do? I panicked. Little panicky chicken."

The hand dropped and finally she lifted her face to him. She looked lost and afraid. "I'm so confused, Sam. I don't know what to do after tonight. All I knew is that I basically took a stick of dynamite to a building I've been working on for years and years, and in two minutes, blew it up to smithereens. Woosh. Boom." Her head shook, working a lock of hair loose. "I still don't understand why I did it."

"I do," he said, his voice hoarse with need. He sat beside her on the bed, took her head and laid it on his shoulder. "And I think you do too."

She burrowed in the space between shoulder and chest and shut her eyes, letting her nerves and worries be soothed by Sam's closeness. Her arms wrapping around his body, she shut her eyes tight and breathed in the clean, soap-and-water scent of him. The smell flooded her mind with memories of the past, so many of them, half-buried in vain but unearthed now and rocking her with their power and potency.

There was one night, a month into their relationship, when they burrowed under an old duvet because her apartment's heater couldn't cope with the cold. At first they were tickling and snuggling and playing around, but then the mood turned serious. Under the blanket it had felt like a story, like kids playacting their deepest secrets and thoughts. Consuelo found herself pouring her heart out to him: how she had been brought up and drilled with the De la Red mythos, her family's grand history and tradition. She described slowly realizing that she didn't really buy it, not really, and that in time she began to think differently of the relatives she'd been taught to scoff. Free from the burden of the family name they had long ago packed up and moved to greener pastures, living mundane lives unencumbered by the pressure to live up to a dead past. She decided she envied them and wanted what they had. It was the first time she said those thoughts out loud, and Sam had listened patiently, letting her speak, no judgments, no opinions.

One morning before spring break: she had just finished a call with her mother, who had been in a paranoid mood and spent the entire two-hour conversation haranguing Consuelo to give up De Paul and just come home. She was angry and annoyed, at herself, more than anyone, because it had seemed so easy to just agree and do what her mother wanted. So she lashed out at Sam, turning their camping trip into an exercise in feminine hostility, but Sam would have none of it. He yelled back when she raged and called her out on what exactly it was that she was doing. And then, somehow, he made her feel like it was all right, and that he had it all in control.

Memories, so many of them, of a year spent together, of a promise that she had allowed to be hijacked from her grasp, because she was too afraid and unsure and unsteady to make a stand.

She breathed his scent once again and sighed. "I wish I could stay here forever," she whispered.

"So do I."

His palm ghosted a caress on her cheek, and then her jaw; his fingers found her chin and tilted it up to meet his lips. This time she was ready for his kiss.

Their earlier kiss in the hallway in front of her room was rough and desperate and ragged. This kiss was slow and sweet, and comforting; holding in it the refuge both so avidly sought. His mouth traced her lips and her tongue followed his lead, teasing and tasting and savoring.

Suddenly desire took hold of her and she trembled with the force of her arousal. Her hands moved from his waist and grabbed his hair, and then she pressed her body tight against his and deepened the kiss. His answering groan and the tightening of his hand against her bare back sent shockwaves through her body, and she bit his lip in return.

His hand traveled up and down her spine, losing all finesse now. His touch was greedy and yearning and unsatisfied, and her lips followed suit, hungry to taste his jaw and his neck and everything else they could get at.

"Gorgeous," he gasped as she kissed and sucked his neck, her hands feverishly unbuttoning his shirt. The last few buttons refused to cooperate with her racing fingers and she growled and ripped the shirt open in frustration.

"Gorgeous!" he cried, heat rising at the sight of Consuelo moving to straddle him, color high in her cheeks, her eyes clouded with desire. She pulled his shirt open and raked her nails over his bare chest, the expression on her face alive with lust. He took her by the waist, pulled her skirt up and settled her over his straining cock. She began to rock against it, the pleasure from the motion of hard cock and textured lace against her aching pussy flooding her entire body, and she bent down to kiss a path from Sam's chest to belly. Her tongue swirled over the sensitive skin just above his belt as her hands traveled up and pinched his nipples.

He moved to pull her up for a kiss, but she shook her head and pushed his chest back down. She wriggled against him and knelt on the floor between his knees. Now her hands dropped to his waist and worked on unbuckling his belt. Sam realized what was she was planning and propped himself on his elbows to watch.

Her movements slowed down now. They were deliberate and languorous as she undid the button on his trousers and slowly unzipped him. She looked up and her expression was so wicked, so full of promise of the things she had in store for him that Sam groaned and raised his hips to help her pull his pants and underwear off.

"Mm," she purred, stroking his huge, throbbing cock. The weight of it was warm and welcome in her hands, and she ran them up and down its length, relishing how Sam threw his head back and closed his eyes. "Did you miss me?" she said, her mouth a hairsbreadth from his shaft, the whisper of her lips eliciting a low moan from him. "I asked," she said, her tongue darting out and slowly licking his length, "did you miss me?" She laughed as he gasped, and then took him in her mouth and sucked.

"God, Sue!" said Sam. He fought to open his eyes and watch but his mind was consumed by the feel of her mouth traveling from head to base, up and down and turning his world into fire and lust. He felt her tongue swirl and caress around the head and then trace the vein along the shaft as the pressure from her sucking threatened to undo him. He grasped her hair and followed the rhythmic, primal motion of her head.

She laughed as she pleasured him, a deep, throaty sound that sent vibrations through his cock and up his belly, and this time it was almost too much. He could almost come, right now, fucking her mouth, but he didn't want to, not yet, so he jerked away and pushed her shoulders back.

The sight of her as she sat on her heels and looked up at him, mouth puffy and eyes heavy-lidded, hair a wild mass over her avid face, was like a kick to the heart. Quick as a panther he pulled her up and placed her over his erection, grinding against her sweet dampness.

"Do you like that?" he said, loving the sight and sound of her, her whimpers and gasps music to his ears. He hurried to remove his ruined shirt then sought to hunt for the brass button that held her dress together—the tiny nub at the base of her nape that had been driving him wild all night, knowing it was all that stood before her and indecency. Finding it, he snapped it off. The halter bodice fell with a slither and an almost audible whisper from her body.

He stopped to take in the sight. All the years, all the long nights filled with flashes of remembering her writhing beneath him; mental pictures of every detail of her naked body; every cherished thought and fantasy paled in comparison of the flesh and blood woman astride him, topless and flushed and in bloom.

But she wouldn't permit him to linger appreciatively any longer. She began to rock against him again, and he could feel how wet she was, even the through the fabric of her thong. Seized with a longing so pitched it was almost painful, he pulled the dress over her head and let his questing hands roam all over her naked body.

Their mouths met again, the kisses hotter than ever, their hands eager to touch and squeeze and stroke and scratch. Sam lifted her hips, their lips still locked, and lay her on the bed, where he could lavish her with the attention he craved to give. He broke their kiss and let his mouth wander, starting from her jaw, down her neck, and across her collarbone. He spent time on her shoulders before following the urges of her arching back and her hand pushing his neck to settle his lips on her breasts.

He gave them all his concentration, these breasts, kissing and licking and fondling and sucking them as though he was conducting an orchestra and Consuelo's moans and sighs were the symphony. He let his teeth graze her nipple, one first, and then the other, and the hips rising from the bed to rub against his thigh was all the approval he needed.

"Sam," Consuelo begged, gripping his neck once again, her other hand traveling down to ease the ache in her core. "Oh!" she gasped, playing with herself, and Sam watched, the lust in him kicking up a notch so that he bit her rib and trailed his teeth across her abdomen.

The brief sharp pain drew another loud gasp from her, heightening their desire and pleasure. Her hips lifted from the mattress again, but this time Sam caught them and pinned them to the bed.

"My turn," he said savagely, favoring her with a grin full of promise. His hand traveled to part her thighs and feel her exquisite wetness, using his thumb to press on her clit so that he had her biting her lip and scratching the duvet in ecstasy. He pressed and pushed another finger inside, then crooked it to find her most sensitive spot, and the cries that were coming out of her now were skirting the edge of control and her head thrashed on the pillow. And then his mouth was on her, and then his tongue, licking her pussy up and down, finding her clit again and teasing it into a pleasure so great Consuelo began to grind against his face.

"Sam—oh! Sam! Please!" she said, moving helplessly, not knowing anything but this delicious feeling inside of her, her mind beyond all sense and reason, her mouth saying things that barely made sense. He licked and licked and her body followed an animal rhythm, older than sense and propriety, oblivious to anything but pleasure. She was close now, so close, he could feel it. She started shivering, starting from her shoulders, the shake building into a crescendo that moved from her belly down to her core before suddenly exploding in orgasm. Her body arched away from the bed from the force of it, her head thrown back to give her pleasure release.

Sam slipped a finger in her again just as she came, savoring the sound of her long scream and the hands frantically clawing at his back. The lust pulled against him, driving him into a frenzy—he just had enough sense to dive to the floor for the wallet in his trousers, dump the contents to find his emergency condom, rip off the foil and sheath himself. When he came back to the bed, he was so crazed with lust that he lifted both her legs against his shoulders and drove into her, sinking his cock to the hilt.

"Fuck, baby!" he said, pumping in and out, the muscles on his arms tense as they carried his weight on top of her. "Yes, yes," Consuelo said, again and again, moving her body to meet his thrusts, each collision sending sparks of lust all throughout each other's body. "Harder," she moaned, and he obliged, driving in and out desperately, forcefully.

He pulled out and rolled her on her belly. Thrilled and frenzied, she went on all fours and cried out when he entered her from behind. He pumped in and out, grasping her ass even as she braced her hands against the wall above the bed and drove against him.

"Oh Sue, oh, oh Sue!" he said, a litany, a prayer, as his mind slowly dissolved. She shoved harder against him as he thrust faster and faster; their movements almost violent as they both ascended and claimed their release. His gasps became more rapid as her cries drove to a climax. Just as he was on the cusp her pussy tightened around him as another orgasm hit her. His own pleasure yanked him from the present, driving him towards a release that bent his mind and obliterated time, like a dark star imploding in space.

He kicked the bedcovers to the floor and fell beside her on the bed, stars dancing in his eyes, his own heart jumping rapidly as though he had just run a marathon. Consuelo lay on her chest, facing him, her back slick with sweat. The smile on her face was the picture of satisfaction. He drew and hugged her close, loving the nearness of her, the soft skin under his touch, her breathing in sync with his and the sleepy, contented way she snuggled against him.

They lay that way for a long time. Consuelo's breaths deepened into a slow rhythm, just as they had when she always fell asleep against him all those years ago.

The memory was sweet, but then it left a bitter aftertaste in Sam's mouth. He had held her like this before, and lost her. It seemed like it was destined to happen again.

He buried his face in her hair and squeezed her tight, fighting to overcome the wave that threatened to engulf him. Consuelo must have sensed the change and stirred; she propped herself up on her elbow and took his face in her hand.

"Sam? What's wrong?"

It was a long moment before he spoke.

"Sue," he said, and his eyes closed. The weight of her name on his lips was an anchor in his heart, sinking deep into him and preventing him from moving on.

"Sue," he said again, desperation tinging his voice now. "What I said earlier—that if I could have you this night, and only this night, I would take it?

"Mm?"

"That was a lie."

A cloud passed over her face and her brows knit in worry.

"One night is not enough," he explained, fighting to keep the anguish out from his tone. "I thought I could be with you tonight and get you out of my system; but I was wrong. I was a fool. I've been trying to get you out of my system all these years and I never succeeded. This night is no different."

He held her against his chest so that she wouldn't see the tears welling in his eyes. It was hopeless. Between the two of them Consuelo was always the one who had mastered the art of concealment, of hiding her emotions under a still and calm countenance. He had always been in thrall to his feelings. He had cried for her before, and was met with stony indifference. He wouldn't do it again.

But Consuelo pushed herself off and raised her neck to look him full in the face.

Consuelo gasped. The tears that had only a second ago threatened now flowed, down his cheeks, two small rivulets across the face of the man that she had always, she realized now, and alone, loved. Her thumbs wiped away the tears and then she kissed each cheek before drawing him in an embrace, putting into the gesture all the words she couldn't say, all that she felt that never quite succeeded in making its way out her mouth.

"Come with me," said Sam, gripping her tight.

"Tomorrow. Come with me."

"Sam—"

"Just say yes, Sue. Come with me." His voice started to take on a hopeful bent and his hands grasped her tightly. "We'll go to Hong Kong, spend a few days there, lay low, figure out what to do next. Or not Hong Kong—somewhere else, even. We can get a ticket at the airport, easy. By this time tomorrow you'll be out of here. You'll be with me."

There was such determined optimism in his words that Consuelo found an answering faith in her heart, such as she hadn't felt ever since she had pushed and cajoled her parents into letting her study in Chicago. That girl had been headstrong and rebellious; a frequent headache and topic of complaint in her mother's lunches with the ladies. The friction between what was expected of her and what she wanted to do was constant, a stress point that threatened to wear her down and grind her away to nothing.

She realized that she allowed exactly that to happen: after Chicago, after her dream of a life away from the obligations of home crashed and burned, she was so heartsick and weary of fighting that she had let her parents and elders grind her down to build her back up into the girl they wanted. And she let them, because she was too tired of the friction, because she began to believe the gospel spread against her. Because, for once, she had wanted to see approval in their eyes instead of disappointment.

And where had that gotten her? To this night. To the very edge of what was sure to be a loveless marriage, to a man who barely regarded her with more affection than a sensible business acquisition.

She reached to Sam's face and cupped his cheek, her realization becoming bigger and stronger by what had just passed between them.

What would happen now? Did she have the strength,

after years of living by proxy, to translate her resolution to action? Did she have the courage to do what Sam asked?

"Just say yes," Sam repeated.

"I want to, Sam," she said. "I really do."

"So what's sto—"

"Just don't ask me to make a decision now, at this moment. I need to think about this. I need to weigh the options."

"What do you need to weigh?" he asked. "What else is left for you here? You said so yourself, back at Lincoln Park, that Manila is basically one big neighborhood with everyone's noses in each other's business. You think you can jump ship here and expect to disappear? You think you won't be sucked into all of this again in a few weeks?"

She turned away, finding his words hard to swallow even as they made sense.

"As long as you stay here, Sue, nothing will change. Your mom will find some other suitable match to pair up with you. Maybe you'll be happy with whoever the fuck that is, maybe you won't. But don't you want to make that choice yourself?"

Consuelo bit her lip and moved to speak, but Sam touched his forehead to hers and cradled her cheeks. She was warm in his arms, naked and open as she would ever be. Whatever passed between them this night seemed to have torn her defenses down. For Sam, all that had happened since they shook hands at the ballroom, and seeing for himself the precariousness of Consuelo's position, made him appreciate the great effort her display of vulnerability was to him. The realization hit him hard and succeeded in untangling the snagged thoughts in his mind.

"I still believe the last words I ever said to you in Chicago," he said, the memory of the park smarting like a reopened wound. "It's your life, Sue; don't let someone else live it for you."

His eyes shut tight and his mouth set in a grim line; his

hands trembled as he sought to steel himself for what he was going to say next.

"I believe in it so much that I won't ask you to make your choice right now."

"Do you really mean that?" Her eyes flew open as she sucked in a breath. She held his face and looked deep into his eyes to search for the truth of what he said. She read it plainly in his pained gaze. He would let her go and leave her to her choice.

"I do, Sue," he said. "I do." His breath left him in a rush as she pulled him for a tight, grateful hug. When they parted he held her at arm's length to take a long, searching look at her face. Depending on what tomorrow would bring, it could be the last he would see of her.

"My flight leaves at noon," he said. "I'll be waiting at the airport curb before then. If you decide to come with me, you'll find me there."

He kissed her again, and his kiss was gentle and full of sorrow, as if the decision was already made, and this was their kiss goodbye. After a moment that seemed to stretch for ages, and right before the kiss heated up into something neither of them would be powerful enough to stop, he drew back and said, "I think you need to get back and face the music."

It was the last thing he said to her that night.

9

Consuelo's eyes flew open and she roused herself with a jolt. The first thing that registered was the chink of yellow light slicing through the hotel room's thick drapes, the brightness proclaiming the lateness of the morning.

"Shit," she muttered, slamming her mobile on the end table when it confirmed that it was already half past nine. She flew off the bed and across the room to the bathroom.

"Shit, shit, shit!" She hadn't planned on sleeping in—she hadn't planned on sleeping at all.

She certainly didn't think sleep was possible after what had happened since she had slunk out of Sam's room, her gown hastily tied by the neck after she failed to recover the brass button he'd popped off. The elevator ride to her floor had been a nerve-wracking exercise in telepathically preventing other guests from meeting the hotel owner's fiancé in all her post-coital walk-of-shame glory, but thankfully no one shared the car with her. Her luck held in the hallway to her suite, although the sounds of the party in full swing did nothing for the shredded state of her nerves.

She rushed to her suite, stripped, and then dipped into a warm, calming bath, letting her hands swirl in the water, mirroring the thoughts churning in her mind. A few minutes, however, into her meditation, her luck finally ran out.

BANG BANG BANG!

The door seemed near to breaking from the force of the violent knocking, and moments later her father's walrus bellows joined the cacophony.

"Come out and talk to me, young lady!" Rudy De la Red screamed, the room's soundproofing no match for his booming voice. An instinctive fear gripped Consuelo; in that split-second she was transformed from an adult woman into a cowering child, dreading her father's wrath and deathly afraid of the crack of his leather belt.

Jumping up she shrugged on a bathrobe, water sloshing on the bathroom floor and then on the carpet as shaking legs brought her to the room's door. Her hand closed on the door knob, but she froze on the spot.

"Consuelo Maria De la Red, open the door, NOW! I know you're in there! Someone saw you come in. Don't pretend you're not there!"

"Rudy, Rudy! Calm down, please, the guests—"

"No, Concha! This girl needs to speak with me now. I will not have her disappearing right when I want a word with her. Open the door, Consuelo!"

"Please, Rudy—"

"Open the door, or so help me—"

The terrible thuds on the door jarred Consuelo from inaction. Something rose inside to strike like an animal threatened, and she heard herself scream: "Or what? Or what will you do to me, Papa?"

There was a moment of stunned silence and then Rudy bellowed once again: "WHAT DID YOU SAY TO ME, GIRL?"

"Are you going to hit me, Papa? Will you beat me until I do what you say?" She shook from head to foot with the force of her words, emotion flowing so intense and so powerful that she seemed to vibrate in its wake. All the years she'd spent saying 'Yes Papa. Of course, Papa' seemed to fly in her face; all her resentment at being treated like a child and prevented from pursuing her own way welled up inside her. "Do it. I dare you!" she exploded. When she heard her father sputter, her leg suddenly flew to kick the door, violent challenge to violent challenge. "Come on, old man, do it! Do it! DO IT!"

"Conchita, stop!" her mother cried. "Open the door, darling, please!"

"No," she answered, letting loose with another swift, hard kick. Her feet hurt but the pain was another form of release, and at this moment Consuelo was all about release. "I will open the door when I feel like opening the door, and you will never tell me what to do again."

Her father began screaming unintelligibly, a primal verbal barrage. The unfocused rage that had flown out of her moments before solidified; inside her the scattered realizations crystallized into action. She stood against the door, feeling the resolve strengthen and course through her veins, and she waited.

Another pair of footsteps joined her parents,' and then came Benjo's unmistakably discreet, cajoling tones against the door. There was a quiet discussion on the other side, too low for her to make out, and she clenched her fists as it stretched over a few minutes. And then—just as she thought Benjo would call his henchmen (he had to have them, didn't he?) to break down the door—footsteps began to move and slowly recede from her hearing.

She stood, tense and animal-alert, against the door; so sure she was of door-breaking henchmen. After several minutes she forced herself to move to the bed, still so tense every little creak and shuffle made her jump. Eventually, however, exhaustion overpowered her, and before she was even aware of it, she had fallen into a deep slumber.

And now she was awake and running around like a headless chicken. She rushed to put on yesterday's jeans and t-shirt and jabbed '0' on the room phone.

"Palace Hotel, may I help you?"

"Yes. This is Consuelo De la Red," she wrestled with the phone and stuffed her feet into her flats at the same time. "I want a hotel car. Now."

"Right away ma'am. Destination?"

She thought for a moment, and then gave her home address.

As the chipper front desk lady asked her if that would be all, she added: "Mr. and Mrs. De la Red, in the adjoining suite—do you happen to know if they're in the hotel?"

"Yes Ma'am. In the outdoor café with Mr. Yu."

"Great. Thank you."

She grabbed her purse, raked her wild hair into a bun, and walked out the room. Everything else— her gigantic overnight bag, the button-less green gown, the tray of accessories and extra pairs of formal shoes—she left behind.

By the time she got to the lobby doors and inside the hotel car she was breathless, having flown through the steps just like Cinderella, if Cinderella was hell-bent on escaping from her Prince Charming. The uniformed driver was chatty, at first, until she silenced him with a haughty word.

And then the fidgeting and lip-chewing began. They were making good time, but the drive seemed too leisurely and less urgent somehow; as if the driver should drive like Evel Knievel to adequately mirror Consuelo's emotions. She almost wished for him to start talking again to distract from the soaring-then-plunging feeling in her belly, her racing heart, her limbs traveling restlessly in the backseat. The trouble was that so many minutes had passed since her rude awakening, and it seemed that time was running out. The resolution that was so crystalline in her mind the night before seemed in danger of shattering, and she looked inward, studying it, turning it over and holding it to the light, so much so that she was blind to the world outside the car windows.

"Left or right, ma'am?" said the driver. It took her a minute or so to realize that they were at her subdivision's gates. With a jump she said "right" and spoke to the guards to let the car through. She guided the driver to her house, all the while feeling her heart kick in her chest and her palms turn moist with sweat.

"Here, ma'am?" he said as they pulled up to the black gate, replete with swirling black ironwork.

Consuelo took a moment to steady herself as she faced her home. It had belonged to her grandfather and then passed on to his son; the house her father grew up in and where she did as well. Even now, with her grandparents long gone, the house still oozed with their presence. It had, she realized, never felt like her home, like a place she belonged; it was the family home, and she only stayed there.

"Wait here," she told the driver.

"Ma'am?"

"Wait for me here." She flung the door and then the gate open and ran all the way inside the house and to her room.

The driver sat back in his chair and pulled off his cap to wipe off the sweat from his forehead. These rich girls and their demands, he thought; they acted like everyone was at their beck and call. This one, Sir Benjo's official girlfriend, was haughty and proud; but maybe it was only because he was comparing her with the flirty, boozy, friendly women his employer asked him to pick up and drop off from time to time.

He wondered where this girl wanted to go next. It was near ten in the morning and he was already hungry; he had woken late and shoved a few pieces of *pandesal* in his mouth as he rushed out the door instead of his usual rice and egg with smoked fish.

His fingers drummed against the steering wheel. Dammit; how long was this girl going to take? His stomach rumbled as he pictured a nice, big hot bowl of *goto*—tasty, garlicky rice porridge with tripe and hopefully a plump hard-boiled egg nestling inside to seal the deal. There was a *gotohan* by the highway entrance on the way back to the hotel; surely he wouldn't be missed for the thirty minutes he'd take to get it in?

The gate creaked open and the girl climbed back into the door, a backpack shrugged over her shoulder.

"Where to, miss?"

"The airport."

"Ah. But ma'am, I can't—"

She waved a crisp thousand-peso bill in the space above the stickshift. "Does this cover it?"

He took it, folded it and slipped it into his pocket. "Yes ma'am."

"And be quick," she said. He obeyed, putting the car in gear.

Eager to impress the rich girl, he pumped the gas as soon as they cleared the subdivision gates and never let his foot off the pedal all the way to the airport. He deftly swerved between lanes, dodged cars, maneuvered behind slow motorcycles and applied every skill in his arsenal to earn the money she gave him. Sure, he was going to be late getting back to the hotel, but one did not just accept thousand-peso bills without exchanging a little service for it, did they?

They pulled up to the airport and idled on the curb. The driver waited for the girl to get out, but a glance in the rear-view mirror showed that she was hesitating, a hand on the door handle, looking like she was searching for someone.

"Ma'am?" he said, wanting to help this sad little rich girl with the morose eyes and frowning lips.

She sighed and dropped her head.

"Ma'am?" he said again. She looked up at him, but

then her features began to brighten and clear. Her gaze moved from him to the windshield, and now a smile broke over her face like a rising sun.

"Thank you, sir!" she said, squeezing his shoulder and then bounding out the door, to the curb and into the arms of the man he had glimpsed from the windshield, a tall man who looked like one of Sir Benjo's contractors or architects. He got out to shut the door the girl had left open, and then drove off; his mind replaying the long, almost embarrassingly passionate kiss between the girl and the contractor-or-architect guy.

"Rich people," he muttered to himself, shaking his head as he drove back to The Palace Hotel.

WHAT HAPPENS NEXT?

Read on to find out what happens to Sam and Consuelo in *One Night In The Streets Of Makati*. Originally published in the #romanceclass Christmas anthology *Make My Wish Come True*, this short story is about Consuelo's best friend Cora (remember her?) but features a cameo from our *One Night At The Palace Hotel* couple. Hope you enjoy it!

One Night In The Streets Of Makati

1

Cora Ciacho loved and missed her best friend, but at this very moment, she wanted to strangle her.

It was Friday night at a speakeasy in Makati—a darkened, tufted, backlit room accessible through a restaurant's emergency exit. She huddled in the darkest barstool, but a gaggle of strangers still pressed around her.

There was a girl with a bob so sharp, it could cut cheese, a man with a shaved head and pockmarked cheeks, and a short, chubby guy in a navy blazer and Chuck Taylors.

"Do you get to keep the clothes from the shoot?" said the girl. What was her name—Therese? Teresa? "The gown you wore on the cover was gorgeous!"

Cora was just about to open her mouth to say no, when the guy with the shaved head cut in: "Is it true that the Carthas brand is expanding to Hong Kong? Are you sure it's wise to compete against the chains there?"

"That's, um," she got out, "but—"

"—I heard that too," said the short guy. "Ciacho Group is going overseas, right? That's why you're onboard."

"Er—"

"Frank," the short guy supplied with a tip of his beer.

"Frank." She really needed to up her name recall game

if *this* was any indication of what life would be like now. Post shareholders meeting. Post announcement. Post the goddamn *Tatler* cover that her father had pushed her to do.

There was a sense of water rising to her ears. Her chest contracted.

She took a deep breath and reached within herself for the spin.

"Let's just say that my father is a very strategic man and he has quite the gift for telling the future," Cora replied smoothly. "Whatever is happening now with the Ciacho Group is, I assure you, very much planned. It will all make sense in due course." She grinned and raised her Jack and Coke. "If you'll excuse me?"

At the front of the room was her best friend Consuelo de la Red, chatting animatedly to a group of well-wishers. Con looked gorgeous, what with her dark curls, rosebud mouth, and haughty *mestiza* features. But right now, she was more than pretty. She glowed as if kindled by an inner fire.

Con's arm snaked through the elbow of the sharply dressed broad-shouldered man. Sam *freaking* Jose. The man responsible for pulling Con away from Manila. The same man who, to be fair, sparked that glow within her friend. She watched as Con paused and met his eyes with a look of complete tenderness, then exchanged a quick but dizzying kiss. The wink of a diamond ring sparkled in the gloomy room as Con's hand cradled his cheek.

"Cora!" Con said, spotting her.

"Con," Cora greeted, bussing her on the cheek. She turned to her friend's fiancé. "Sam."

He nodded coolly. He had good reason to be cold to her, what with her being one of the reasons he and Con had broken up the first time in Chicago.

Con caught his look with a quick laugh. "Oh my gosh, you two. Bury the hatchet!"

"There's no hatchet to bury!" Cora exclaimed at the same time as Sam said, "What hatchet are you talking about?"

"Look," Con rolled her eyes. "All's well that ends well and that was nine freaking years ago. Shake hands."

"You're not actually making us do this," Cora scoffed.

"Shake. Hands," Con replied dangerously.

"Fine." He thrust his hand out. "I forgive you for ratting out Sue to her parents when she had you sworn to secrecy, which, as we all know now, turned out to be a false alarm."

She deserved that, but still winced. "I'm sorry," she said. "And *I* forgive you for turning Consuelo here into this scary, bossy monster."

She emphasized Con's full name—she could never get used to how Sam called her oldest friend "Sue."

"That's not me; that's Hong Kong."

"Yes, Cora, give me some credit! Being Sam's trophy girlfriend has toughened me up."

Sam choked on his whiskey. Con reached up and helpfully thumped him on the back. "He hates it when I call myself that," she said sweetly.

"It makes me feel like a dirty old man, Sue," he frowned. "Like I take you around to meet clients just for them to have something beautiful to look at."

"Oh but I don't mind," she batted her eyelashes. "It works for us when they underestimate me. It completely blindsides them when I push your asking price."

His frown turned into a look of pure admiration. "They never know what hits them, do they, Gorgeous?"

The heated gaze between them made Cora feel uneasy, like her skin was a size too small. She coughed discreetly and Con laughed.

"I keep asking Sue to make it official, work-wise," said Sam, eyes still glued on his would-be wife. "The firm is small; we can definitely add a Director for Corporate Liaisons."

"And go to the office every day?" Con wrinkled her pert nose. "I don't think so. Leave me to the parties and the schmoozing. Besides," she slid her hand under his jacket and over his chest. "You can't afford me."

"Good thing you take other things as payment."

They kissed again, so long and lusty that Cora felt her knees go a little weak. "Guys…?"

"Sorry, Cora," said Con, licking her lips.

"*I'm* not apologizing for that," said Sam with a smug grin. "But I need to leave you ladies. Steph's just arrived—haven't seen him in ages."

"Well, congratulations, Consuelo de la Red." Cora grasped her best friend's hands as he left. "I'm really happy for you."

"Are you?" The self-satisfied expression left Con's face and desperate hope flooded her large brown eyes.

"Of course I am," she reassured her. "I truly, really am."

Con squeezed her back and let out a shaky breath. "You have no idea how great that is to hear, Cora."

She didn't want to ask, but best friend duties mandated otherwise. "I take it Tito and Tita aren't coming?"

Con shook her head. "There's a reason why our engagement party is in a secret bar hidden behind a restaurant's emergency exit, Cora."

"Oh, Con." She hugged her quickly. "Why did you have to have your engagement party here, anyway? I could've flown to Hong Kong, no problem."

"To reconnect with everyone, silly," Con sniffed against her shoulder. "We haven't been back in three years. Was it too naïve of me to think that things could have been patched up by now?"

"I'm sorry," she said.

"Don't be," said Con. "Just don't slink out while my back is turned like I know you're planning." Cora blanched and sputtered while Con batted all-knowing doe eyes. "I know you, *betch*."

"You do, *betch*," Cora raised an eyebrow as Con

giggled over their silly schoolgirl nickname. "You tricked me into coming here. '*Oh, Cor, I miss you, it's just a small dinner.*' I walk in and it's a goddamn engagement party!"

"I know you wouldn't come otherwise and this is our only free night in Manila." She pushed a fresh cocktail from a passing waiter into Cora's hand. "It's not my fault you're now a bigshot heiress tycoon with her own *Tatler* cover."

She felt a hot stab of anxiety. For a few moments she had forgotten the *Tatler* cover; now it was thrust back into her mind's eye:

The gown of navy blue lace, the heavy makeup, the fake lashes that made her eyelids droop.

The goddamn headline.

Her Father's Daughter
Cora Ciacho on finally stepping up and taking the reins

She grimaced at that backhanded *finally*. If only those pithy headline writers knew.

"Don't bother with 'If they only knew,' *Cora,"* her father would say. "*They will never know. Use their assumptions—work with it or use it against them.*"

She took another deep breath and a sip of her new cocktail. "Shut up, *betch*. Go to your adoring fans," she gestured toward the door, where a fresh wave of well-wishers entered.

Con squeezed her arms, motioned her to stay put and blew her a kiss.

Cora dropped to a vacant seat with a sigh, resigned to making nice for another thirty minutes, max, before she could get back to her condo and soak her aching feet in the home foot spa her sister Cherry had gotten her as a gag birthday gift (which she secretly loved).

No sooner had she sat when a stocky guy sidled up to her. "Did you by any chance take your MBA at NUS?" he asked with an all-too-open smile.

She held in a groan and grinned back.

2

Cora Ciacho was being propositioned across the room, and Stephen Cruz was feeling conflicted about it.

He hated that he knew who she was. He took a perverse pride in not being updated on "personalities"—people famous for being famous, or in Cora's case, filthy rich.

But just that morning he had found himself at a Starbucks behind a woman who'd ordered twelve venti berry panna cotta frappuccinos and then demanded an overly complicated official receipt. He had no choice but to pick up the society magazine strewn on an empty table as he waited for his grande triple latte.

There she was on the cover: *Her father's daughter.*

Though he didn't keep up with "personalities," *everyone* knew the name Ciacho. The family had a cargo company, a shipping line, and a recently opened budget airline. They also owned payment and remittance centers and a string of department stores in Visayas and Mindanao.

So this was the girl who stood to get it all. He had stared at her magazine cover for quite a while, taken in by the interesting expression on her face. Beneath the thick eyelashes and come-hither makeup, she wore a look that was almost...fearful. Like she was just waiting for the piano to fall on her head.

Why would a girl who had everything have that expression on her magazine cover?

She was not looking so fearful now. Her long legs, tucked inside soft, silken trousers, were angled away from the square-bodied guy who was taking up all available table space. She held her cocktail protectively, her elbow pointing towards his chest, and while she smiled, it did not quite reach her eyes, which every now and then swept across the room as if looking for rescue.

Sam, his favorite *amboy* cousin, was being coaxed to down shots of Patrón by the bar, while his cousin's fiancée was shrieking at the opposite end of the room at a phone held to her face.

Stephen groaned inwardly. Cora looked truly uncomfortable, and the guy harassing her didn't seem to take the hint.

He sidled over to her table with a confident smile he did not feel.

"There you are!" he said. "Our ride is here."

She slowly turned toward him, a jagged line between her brows as she no doubt wondered who the hell he was.

Please take the hint. Please take the hint.

"What?" she asked, with a voice that cracked like a whip.

"Our ride. Your driver," he answered, grinning a little too much, widening his eyes in the hopes that she could maybe see past his eyeballs into his brain, where he was flashing this neon sign: *I'm trying to rescue you, woman!*

The jagged line gradually smoothed out. "Ohhhh." Her own eyes went round. "*That* took long enough."

"I know, right!" He tried his mightiest not to giggle like a fool. "But the traffic is terrible."

"Riiighttt…" she drawled, turning to the stocky guy who'd been bugging her. "I'm sorry…?"

"Ed."

"Yes. Ed. Well." She smiled and grasped Stephen's

arm.

Through his jacket he could feel her fingers shaking gently. A surge of protectiveness overpowered him, and before he could question himself, he covered her hand with his own. There was a small moment when her eyes dropped to his hand, but she quickly covered that up with a smile toward Clueless Ed.

"It was nice meeting you." Her inflection almost made that sound like a question.

Then she went to the door, hand still firmly clamped around Stephen's arm. They parted the heavy curtains that hid the speakeasy from the short, dark hallway behind the emergency exit. Cora's grip tightened as they entered the suffocating dark. Stephen pushed the exit door and heard her take a deep breath as they found themselves in the brightly lit restaurant.

He thought she would drop her hand and leave, but her grip did not relax, and she led him across the restaurant floor, out the door to the Makati City sidewalk, beneath the slight December evening chill.

Under the streetlight, Cora fumbled in her clutch for a squashed pack of cigarettes and a plastic lighter. She jammed a stick into her mouth and tried to light it with still shaking fingers.

"Here," said Stephen, coaxing a flame from the sputtering barrel. She took a deep drag and exhaled slowly.

"Thanks."

"You're welcome."

"So. Um." He scuffed the toes of his shoes on the pavement and cast around for something to say. "How do you know Sam and Sue?"

"Consuelo and I have been best friends from grade school."

"Ah. Sam is my. Um. Cousin."

"Nice," she said icily. She took another deep puff.

"Do you always smoke?"

Her eyebrow arched. "Do you care?"

"I was just asking."

Her expression softened a fraction. "I'm trying to quit. But stressful situations…" she waved her cigarette toward the restaurant. "Thanks for that, by the way."

"No problem," he answered. "You looked like you needed rescuing."

Her face hardened again. "*I* don't need any rescuing, thank you very much."

The tips of his ears burned. "In that case, you wouldn't mind if I step back in there and tell Ed I don't really know you and the ride thing was a lie?"

"You wouldn't." Her almond-shaped eyes widened in alarm.

"I wouldn't," he admitted, scratching the back of his head. "Um. You don't like a free excuse to escape an unwanted conversation?"

"I didn't like your choice of words," she said with a thrust of her chin. "But I did thank you."

He felt another flash of embarrassment. Being around her was making him even more awkward than usual.

"I'm sorry. I tend to say the wrong things all the time. I only meant to help. I didn't mean to imply you were some damsel in distress."

Watching her now, all long, spare limbs in soft white clothes, *chinita* eyes narrowed suspiciously against the cigarette smoke, the image that came to mind wasn't a damsel in distress.

No. What came to his mind were the sharp planes of her jaw and cheeks as her red mouth opened in ecstasy while he—

Stop it, Stephen.

"Sorry for snapping at you," she said softly. "*That* in there…it's not my thing."

"No problem," he said again. He watched her as she took another long drag and absently stared at the lantern-hung streetlights.

God. Say something.

"I'm Stephen, by the way. Stephen Cruz."

She raised her eyebrows but didn't reply.

"And you are…?" he prompted, then winced. *He* knew who she was. He just didn't know how else to fill the silence.

A brief look of disbelief crossed her features. "I'm…Cora," she offered her hand. "Cora Ciacho?"

She was checking whether he really was a doofus who had no idea who she was. Stephen quickly ran through two possible courses of action.

If he admitted that he did know who she was, he'd probably blurt out that he had just been skimming her *Tatler* cover story earlier that day, which meant he would be then forced to admit that he asked for her name out of sheer unimaginative awkwardness. She could conclude that he had led her out of the party just so he could have a conversation with her away from everyone else jockeying for her attention. Or worse, decide that he was a weirdo.

If he played it cool and pretended he really did not have any idea who she was, that would make sense within the parameters set by his earlier name-asking.

He nodded to himself and said:

"Nice to meet you, Cora."

She shook his hands, her eyes round with surprise. Then the disbelief in them slowly turned into delight, and the penny dropped for Stephen.

She did *not* want to be recognized. It didn't matter that he was a doofus who didn't know who she was. This actually worked for her.

"So, Stephen Cruz. What next?"

"I'm sorry?"

He must've goggled because she explained patiently, "We just invented a bogus excuse to get away from that guy and now neither of us can get back in because it's going to be completely obvious that we lied."

"So…we each go home?" he volunteered.

"Oh," she blinked rapidly.

"I mean—"

God, why was this so hard? Here was a beautiful woman who seemed to want to spend a bit more time with him. But he had no idea what to do, and any suggestion sounded too forward in his head. Besides, though it was late, it was not late enough for traffic to thin out. Three days before Christmas Eve, the rush hour stretched out to midnight and the streets were snarled with cars that hadn't moved an inch the entire time they were talking.

"Do you live nearby? I don't think we'll get a ride anytime soon. I can walk you home or—?"

"My place isn't close, but it's walkable."

"Just point me in the right direction."

She crushed the cigarette under her spiky heel. "Tell you what. Instead of walking 10 blocks to my place while I'm wearing these terrible shoes, why don't we grab a bite to eat first? I'm starving."

"That sounds like a good idea," he tamped down a smile that pulled at his cheeks. "What are you in the mood for?"

"Soup, maybe?" She looked across the street, to the closing mall. "Not there, obviously."

"I know where we can go."

He felt bold. Adventurous. A teensy bit reckless. He had rescued (never mind if she didn't like the word) her from…an insufferable conversation. And now she was asking him to soup. To soup!

So he took it another step and grasped her slim hand. He waited for a split second for her to protest; and, when she did not pull back, led her across the street.

3

He was a funny boy.

Slim, in that fine-boned way that she liked, and tall, but not in the way that made her feel like he loomed over her. He had a boyish, innocent face, complete with a deep dimple in one cheek. He needed a haircut. She liked that his eyes looked kind and almost a little pained, like he was always on the verge of apologizing for something.

She grasped his hand as they threaded through the snarled mass of cars and crossed into the dark side street between the mall and a row of mid-rise condominiums. His hand was warm and steady as they emerged on a cobblestoned walkway and turned to the sidewalk of the city's main thoroughfare. Cars stood bumper to bumper in the late evening, their red brake lights adding a nearly festive air to the scenes of local Christmas traditions picked out in LED fairy lights at the road's island. It was almost magical, if not for the chorus of beeping horns.

Just another pre-Christmas Carmageddon in the old CBD.

"You're taking me to the light show, aren't you," she said to his slim back.

He paused and turned. The side of his face was

sheepish in the multicolored glow of traffic and fairy lights.

"The restaurants there are still open at this time," he explained.

Yeah. Open and crowded.

He must've read the reservation on her face. "I'm sorry. It's just that…I haven't caught the light show yet, and we're so near, and I'm never in Makati."

"You don't work around here?"

"God, no. I'm all the way over at Eastwood."

She winced. "Traffic city."

"Right? And I kind of have…a pact." His face nearly collapsed in embarrassment, and it made her smile with a surge of sympathetic humiliation. "A pact to see the light show every year. And this *may* be the only time I'm ever in this part of the city during the Christmas season."

He looked so earnest too, that against her reservations, she nodded.

He pulled at her hand (how was it possible that they were still holding hands?) and they paused at a narrow pedestrian lane, opened only late at night. Immediately they were surrounded by a large group of people.

"So what do you do over at Eastwood?" she said, trying to fight off the claustrophobia.

He squinted, like he was going to admit something that caused him pain. Then he blurted out:

"I'm a resources manager for a BPO."

"That wasn't too bad, was it?"

"What?"

"You looked embarrassed about sharing it."

"Oh. No." He lifted his other hand and tugged at the hair that brushed his ear. "It's just a little boring, that's all."

"In what way? And compared to what?"

The crowd suddenly surged forward, carrying them along.

"Compared to…most jobs."

"What does a resource manager do, anyway?"

He tugged at his ear again. "Well, you know how a

BPO has, like, a lot of clients and projects? And each of those projects need the right resources—people, obviously, but also equipment like seats, computers, headsets, software. And there are times when projects need more people and others when they need less?"

"Uh-huh."

They reached the courtyard of the stock exchange building, a big, open space with fountains on one end and the park and light show on the other. It was filled with what seemed like a thousand onlookers, spotlights raking over the crowd. Classic OPM hits played in a medley interspersed with Christmas carols. He gently pushed her towards a bit of space between a display of blown up Christmas lanterns, putting himself between her and the crowd. Her breath rushed out in relief.

"My job is to make sure that project needs and site resources balance out just right."

"So you make sure that everyone who comes to work has a computer and a place to sit."

He made that apologetic wince again. "Yes, but it's more complex than that. See, clients pay us for the space they use within our sites, but they also pay for the *time* those spaces are used. Let's say an Australian project starts at six am and ends at three. We'd then have a bunch of idle seats and tables for a good chunk of the day—space we could offer to another client in the UK from four pm to one am, for example. Space is time is money. It's my job to make sure that all those spaces and resources are at maximum capacity without going over the limit, because we don't want two agents sharing a desk and a headset, you know what I mean?" He grinned as she nodded. "Now imagine 57 projects. Some of them asking for more seats on peak months, others reducing when demand slows."

"When you put it that way, it's like you're managing a massive Jenga puzzle."

His eyes shone with delight. "Thank you! Yes, that's

exactly how I feel about it too."

She couldn't help but grin back at his enthusiasm. It almost made her forget to brace for the next question he was sure to ask.

"What about you, what do you do?"

She took a deep breath. It was pointless to lie. He could pop into a convenience store right now and see her face on the magazine rack.

"I'm an heiress."

His open, trusting face went just a little too wide, like an old book cracked open at the spine.

"An heiress?" His voice was airy and high.

"Uh-huh. Ciacho Group of Companies. Let's see: Carthas department stores in Cebu, Bacolod, Iloilo, Dipolog, and General Santos. Also, Pay Cia, Ciacho Shipping, and CiaAir?"

He swallowed hard. "Yeah?"

"All mine. One day."

She had wanted to be breathy and breezy about it, but her voice shook and broke off at the end of "One day." Still, she held it together. She held it together as he seriously and steadily studied her face, the sweeping spotlights picking out the spiky tips of his overgrown haircut.

She held it together until he said:

"I'm sorry."

Suddenly she was blinking very quickly and very hard, studying the toes of her stilettos. Then long arms engulfed her shoulders, and she was pressed against his chest.

His warm chest, solid with firm, lean muscles, smelling of fabric softener and light cologne, thudding with a heartbeat that seemed a little too fast beneath her ear.

She froze at the sudden contact and he released her. She looked up at him, her thoughts a tangled jumble.

A jumble that went something like:

godhesmelledsogoodbutshouldn'tIbemadhehuggedmeohcomeonitwasjustahuggoddamnwhyyyy

Three pings sounded over the loudspeakers. "The show's starting," he said hoarsely, taking her hand in his. He led her quickly through the crowd to a prime position under the sprawling branches of two ancient trees, twined with fairy lights. He scrambled up the cement planter and held out a hand to pull her up.

A hush descended on the crowd as the high, clear notes of a bell sounded, in perfect sync with the flashing shell-shaped lights ringing the boughs of every tree in the park.

The bells turned into a crescendo of tambourines and strings, and the lights traveled from bough to branch, flowing up and then dripping down the leaves in icicle-like cascades of twinkling lights.

She snuck a peek at Stephen's face. It was rapt in captivated wonder, eyes bright as he watched the lights dance and flow and surge in time with the cheery music. She couldn't help but smile. She'd probably watched the Ayala Triangle light show dozens of times, every year, as she sometimes cut across the stock exchange building and through the park to work, so much so that she treated it like background music and the crowds of watchers unwelcome obstacles in her way.

But watching it beside him now, witnessing his obvious delight…

The music built to a sparkling climax and ended to applause.

"Why are you smiling at me like that?" he asked, a little shyly.

"Nothing." Yet she couldn't help but keep grinning.

He hopped off the planter and helped her down, his hands warm on her waist.

The paths were choked with people heading away from the light show or trying for the best positions before it started up again, and they were forced to walk on the grass. Her heels sank into the soft soil but she soldiered on.

"Who'd you make it with?" she asked.

"What?"

"Your pact. You said you have a pact to watch the light show every year. Who'd you make it with?"

This was the third time this evening that he blushed, a darker tan spreading across his cheeks. She was torn between wondering at his perpetual embarrassment and wanting to see that flush on his face again.

"My mother loved the light show." His voice was soft—almost too soft to hear over the din of the crowd. "Remember the first time they ever had it, all those TV and radio commercials? She was so excited, she kept bugging me and my brothers to take her to see it. We kept telling her it was too crowded, the traffic too bad just to see a bunch of Christmas lights. That maybe it wouldn't be good for her...her health."

She bit her lip as his voice wavered at the last word. He struck a nerve deep inside her. She thought of a large bedroom converted into an intensive care unit, of hulking oxygen tanks and the ever-present smell of disinfectant and decay...

"Ma wasn't put off. She was great at Cold War tactics; treated us like air for a whole week. So finally Kuya and I brought her here. She loved it. She was so happy." He smiled, sadly and wistfully. "So the next year, when she wasn't around to see the next light show, I promised I would, for her. I've been coming every year since."

She squeezed his hand, tried to put as much understanding as she could into her touch.

The throng increased despite the late hour. Stephen led her to the end of the restaurant row, looking for the shortest line, but every door was mobbed. Cora couldn't help but whimper. Her feet were sore and her stomach grumbled.

"I can't believe this," she gritted her teeth. "Every place is full! To think that right at this very moment every hotel around here is probably overflowing with soup that's being ignored at Christmas parties. All that good, thick, warm soup being wasted. It makes me mad."

Stephen looked at her funnily.

"Soup. Hot soup," she pressed, more than a little delirious with hunger, frustration, and stiletto pain. "Thick pumpkin soup with little croutons on top. Mushroom soup with bits of shiitake. Cream of spinach. Broccoli and cheese. Oh God."

He wet his lips and looked around.

"The Pen's across the street from here."

She'd been slumping over, but rose to full height at his words.

"You up to a soup rescue, Stephen Cruz?"

4

This was insane.

Stephen sat at the edge of one of the elegant armchairs in the Peninsula's lobby, sweat beading at his temples and under his nose.

Cora Ciacho was a woman obsessed. With rescuing soup.

He'd thought she was joking. When they got to the relative calm of the hotel, he assumed they'd get the blasted soup from the lobby cafe. But the idea of soup ignored at a buffet had riled Cora up somehow, and now she was hell-bent on her plan.

Which was to crash one of the parties happening in the hotel's ballrooms.

There were at least four going on that he could tell from the hotel's announcement boards. The Christmas parties of a small accounting firm and a multi-level marketing company were in the smaller ballrooms, that of a telco in the largest. There was a wedding reception at the Conservatory. He cringed at the traffic awaiting the guests.

"Let's go," said Cora, appearing by his elbow from the ladies' room. She was so sleek and unruffled, it was as if he'd only imagined their frustrated trudge through the

Ayala Triangle Gardens.

She smelled intoxicating too. Like honeysuckle and other things that bloomed at night.

"Which one are we crashing?" he asked, resigned.

"Telco's our best bet," she smiled. "Too many guests to keep track."

He followed her to the Rigodon ballroom with a small sigh. She was a vision in white, the soft fabric of her blouse and pants kissing the long lines of her body, a beautiful contrast to the golden tone of the skin that showed at her elbow and neck. She turned and winked cheekily at him and his heart stopped for a beat.

He was no match for a girl like this. He'd probably rob a bank for her, if she asked.

The registration tables outside the ballroom were unmanned and strewn with sign-up sheets and various paper hats. Fedoras, children's party cones, even one with a little propeller at the crown.

"*Hats Off To The Holidays*," Cora murmured, reading the sign-up sheet. She put on the cardboard fedora and Stephen followed with the propeller hat. "It suits you," she grinned. "If anyone asks, we're from Region IV Marketing, none of whom signed up here." She replaced the sign-up sheets. "And I'll be making sure all Ciacho Group parties do their registration online. *This* is such a security risk."

He gave her an incredulous look as she burst out laughing. "Come on! Soup waits for no one."

It was mayhem inside. The party had clearly been going on for a while now; a show band was playing a blistering cover of a Bruno Mars hit and the dance floor was packed with people in top hats, flower crowns, wedding veils, and striped Dr. Seuss hats. The few tables that were still occupied were laden with half-empty bottles of beer and shotglasses; a crowd near the ballroom's east side mobbed a mobile bar.

"Eek!" Cora shrieked, pulling Stephen to the buffet table. She grabbed a bowl and ladled it from the soup barrel. "Oh my God, it smells like roasted pumpkin," she moaned, then balanced a small plate on her other hand to load it with various antipasti.

They settled into an empty table, furthest from the stage, where it was dark and the noise manageable. A waiter handed them utensils and glasses of iced tea; Cora attacked her soup with relish. She savored every bite, closing her eyes and making little sounds of pleasure that made it hard for him to think.

Literally.

He concentrated on his own bowl, but he couldn't taste anything. His thoughts were focused on what her lips would taste like, if he leaned over to kiss her now. Sweet like pumpkin, perhaps, and an underlying flavor that was all her own.

"Mmm," she said, mopping up the last bits of soup with a dinner roll. "I'm so glad we did this."

"Save soup from being wasted?"

"Uh-huh. We helped it fulfill its destiny. It's home now," she patted her stomach dreamily.

He was so charmed by the sight that his mouth got away from him again.

"I'd never think a girl like you would care so much about wasted soup."

Her face hardened and he instantly regretted opening his stupid mouth.

"Really. And how is a *girl like me* supposed to act?"

He hoped to get away with not answering her question, but her dark eyes pinned his gaze.

"I'm sorry, Cora, I didn't mean—"

"No, Stephen. You did. You have assumptions about me, so let's have it out."

His ears were on fire. "I only meant that, you know, having so much, um..."

"Money."

"Yeah. That. I thought that it wouldn't be a big deal to you if, you know, a tiny bit of it went to waste."

She straightened in her seat and leveled him a cool glare.

"What do you know about my father, Stephen?"

"Your father? Um—"

"My father had to quit school and work when he was 16 to make sure his four siblings were able to finish. They were orphaned, you know. Some nights were so bad, all they had to eat was salt and rice."

He swallowed hard, feeling monumentally stupid.

"When my sister and I were young and we didn't finish our rice, he would have a fit. He would tell us, 'Do you know how hard it is to harvest rice?' And then he would go into detail. We couldn't leave the table until he took us from planting and irrigation and all the way to harvest, where farmers would take whatever cash they made from that season's take and use it to pay off all the debts they accumulated in the previous months. Without the harvest, they didn't have any cash. 'Can you imagine not having any cash?' he'd ask. Then he'd end with 'How do you think farmers would feel, knowing you're throwing away those little grains they nearly kill themselves growing?'"

"I'm sorry, Cora, really. I didn't know."

"Lots of people don't know, but they assume they do." She reached up and pulled off the cardboard fedora. "They think that because I was born rich, everything was handed to me on a silver platter. Do you know what my first job out of college was?"

He shook his head.

"I was a trainee at a pharmaceutical. My father had told me, go work for another company, and if you're good enough to get promoted there, then you're good enough to work for me. He only asked me to join Ciacho when I became assistant manager." She took a shaky sip of iced tea. "Back when I first started working, as soon as I got regularized, he told me I needed to leave the house and get my own place. I had roommates the first four years of my career. Now I live in a 50 square-meter studio. I upgraded when I became a VP.

"I don't have an allowance from my dad. I earn a salary, same as every employee in his company, and I save up just like anyone else when I want something." Her hand toyed with the soup spoon and the ice in her tone thawed a fraction. "The way some of my friends react, it's like I'm being abused or something. But I've always known my father was training me for something big, and that felt safe, you know? It felt like I had boundaries. If I kept inside them, I'd always be fine."

Her dark eyes searched his. "When I told you I was an heiress and that all of Ciacho Group was going to be mine, you told me you were sorry. Why was that?"

He shrugged. "I just thought it was a huge responsibility, handling all of that. Just a lot to take on. I would be scared shitless, if it were me."

She laughed, a sudden, harsh exhale, and then her face crumpled into tears.

"Oh God, how am I doing this? I always say the wrong things." He ran his hand through his hair and then pulled her against his chest. "Shit. I'm sorry. Do you want to be hugged? You don't, do you? Shit, I'm an idiot!"

Her silent sobs turned into shaking laughter. Her own arms wrapped around him.

"Are…are you alright?" he asked, rubbing her back, half feeling like a doofus and half thrilled at having her in his arms.

"You nailed it," she laughed softly against his chest. "That's how I feel. Scared shitless."

She drew back from him and dabbed at her eyes. "Most people assume I'm thrilled to control Ciacho Group. That I can't wait to be so *powerful*." She made spooky spirit fingers at the last word. "But you get me, don't you, Stephen? You don't always say the right things, but you do."

"No more boundaries now?" he guessed.

"Dad is…" she sighed. "It won't be long now. I need to sack up."

He pulled his silly hat off and slowly walked his fingers on the table until he reached her hand. "It's okay to be scared. I think. When you're scared because you understand the size of what you're carrying, and everything that you can affect. That kind of fear means that you...you care. And if you care, that makes you a good leader." He gripped her fingers and grimaced. "I wish I could put it better, but...you get what I mean?"

She nodded. And then, very swiftly, she pushed off the table and kissed him on the cheek. The touch of her lips burned and left him with a lingering trace of her scent.

"What did you really want to say, when you made that quip about a 'girl like me'?"

He winced. "I wasn't really thinking. You were so pleased with your soup and so cute when you patted your tummy, I wanted to make the moment last longer. To say something cool and witty and maybe make you laugh?"

She parted her lips to reply when a girl approached their table, holding a bucket of colorful test tubes on ice.

"Let's gooooo!" trilled the girl, handing them each a test tube. "Shot! Shot!"

Cora accepted a red tube with genuine amusement.

"What is this?" Stephen wrinkled his nose at the blue liquid in his test tube.

Cora downed hers one gulp and made a face. "Whoo! What the hell?"

Stephen followed. "Gah. That tasted like pure gin."

The girl laughed and went to the other table like a demented alcohol peddler. Cora stood and grabbed his arm. "Come on, let's dance!"

They reached the dance floor. The band had finished their set and a DJ was now on stage, spinning hard EDM that was whipping the crowd into a frenzy under the crazy spinning lights. Cora laughed, kicked off her heels, and plunged into the throng.

Stephen followed. The crowd was so thick, they were pushed against each other. He felt every undulation as she moved her hips and shoulders to the music. He placed his hands on her waist—partly to keep her a safe distance from his burgeoning...feelings, and partly to feel her skin against his palms.

She gave into the music, shutting her eyes and letting her body answer the beat. She spun beneath his hands and swung her head, moving her body like a wave that crashed into him. She laughed again and wrapped her arms around his neck.

He let his forehead dropped to hers as their bodies heaved against each other. Their hips collided and her mouth dropped to his lips, a breath away.

God, he wanted to kiss her. His hands tightened around her waist as he mastered his control.

She leaned in and kissed him anyway.

5

He was so funny.

When she put her lips against his, he jerked in surprise. She could almost hear the panicked thoughts in his brain.

But then he found his bearings and kissed her back.

A kiss, she always thought, was like a conversation. You presented yourself to another person and invited them to reveal a little bit of themselves to you.

His kiss was just a little sloppy, just a tad unpolished, just like his hair. But he put himself into the kiss, eagerly and wholeheartedly, with an openness that she could taste from the sweep of his tongue and the softness of his lips. He offered all of himself in that kiss, and it was so heady, so intoxicating, it took her breath away.

The hands on her waist crushed her against him. She felt all his excitement. In abundance.

There was a spell in the tribal beat of the music, the dizzying swirl of lights, the bitter hint of alcohol in his mouth and the heat of his hands now traveling up and down her back. Her mouth drew against his ear and said:

"I think you need to take me home."

They slunk from the dance floor and across the ballroom to pick up her clutch. Outside the hotel, the traffic jam had eased.

"I'm parked a couple of blocks behind the speakeasy," she said, tugging his hand to cross the street.

"Cora?" He looked at her bare feet.

"Shit." She turned back to the hotel entrance.

Stephen shrugged. "I'll carry you."

"What? No!"

He turned and squatted. "Hop onto my back."

"Goddamnit, what if people see us?"

"Why do you say that?"

"Say what?"

"Goddamnit."

She heated. "My maternal grandfather was in the military. Kind of a running joke between my dad and I."

"So are you getting on?"

"I—"

"Hide your face. We'll just pretend you're drunk."

She hesitated for another few seconds, and then climbed onto his back. She clung to his neck and buried her face against it. He rose and strode forward, his strong, warm hands gripping the legs wrapped around his hips.

"This is so embarrassing," she whispered against his neck.

She felt him shudder. "Please don't talk against my neck like that." His voice was hoarse and shaky.

"Why not?"

"It feels too good," he said. "You're going to make me drop you."

She shut up and as he crossed streets and walked down sidewalks, she perched on him like a baby monkey. He was surprisingly strong for such a slim guy; he wasn't even breathing heavily when they neared the parking lot.

She concentrated on the cologne around his neck, the feel of his back muscles as they slid and flexed under her chest and the sound of his breath.

Smell and feel and sound: he was right. This was too good.

"Tell me where," he said, as soon as they entered the gravel parking lot. She directed him until they reached her Toyota sedan.

"An Altis?" he commented wryly.

"You were expecting something more car-nappable?"

He chuckled and tightened his grip.

"You can let me down now," she prompted.

His grip on her loosened and she slid down his back, her feet setting gently on the gravel. The motion felt intimate somehow, the friction of her clothes against his body overwhelming her senses. It took her a while before she could remember how to disarm the alarm, open the doors for them both, and start the car.

She drove for a few blocks in silence.

"You okay, Stephen?" she glanced as she made a turn.

He nodded, the slight apology still in his eyes. She had the overwhelming urge to kiss him on the deep dimple on his cheek. She wanted to replace the reluctance in his eyes with that same enthusiastic openness she had felt in his kiss.

"Please," she said. "Say something."

He blew out a shaky breath.

"What should I say?"

"Anything. Anything to make me feel like...like we're not making a mistake."

"I can't do that."

"Why not?"

"I'm going to say the wrong thing, and *then* it will be a mistake."

The light on an intersection turned red and she took the opportunity to look at him.

The expression on his face was intense. The look on his eyes was deep and dark, like a tunnel toward the feelings that were overpowering him, feelings so strong, words weren't enough—they only failed him.

"Light's green," he murmured, voice inky and sinuous inside the car.

She shifted gear and drove. There was a funny feeling in her belly, the soft fluttering of a hundred butterflies. The skin between her shoulder blades felt cool and sensitive, and between her and Stephen there seemed to be a sparkle of stars ready to ignite at the slightest friction.

"I always have a hard time with words," he finally said. "I can never make them fit around what I really mean."

"Don't shape them." Her own voice was curiously breathless. "Be blunt. What are you thinking about?"

She heard his sharp intake of breath.

"I'm thinking of your kiss," he said. "About how good you tasted, pumpkin and gin and something sweet and deep. I've been wondering how you tasted, ever since I saw you at the speakeasy."

"Really." She concentrated on keeping her eyes on the road.

"Yes. And not just your mouth. I want to know how your skin tastes like."

"M-my skin?"

"It's all soft and golden and smooth. I keep thinking about running my lips over your wrist. On the soft parts near your elbow. Your neck. That hollow between your collarbones...I want to lick it. I'm wondering how you would react, if I touched you there. Tasted you there."

Something clenched deep within her belly. Her breathing stuttered. Two more turns…

"Should I continue?"

"Yes," she sighed. "Keep going."

"I'm wondering if there are parts of you as hard as I am now. Lean forward."

She did as he said, and she heard a low hiss.

"God. Your nipples are poking through your blouse. Ah, yes. I want to lick those too. Lay my tongue flat and feel them against my lips. I'd suck them inside my mouth, those hard little nipples. I bet they're so sensitive now. Aren't they? The feel of your bra and blouse against them is too much."

"D-damnit, Stephen!"

"Are you...are you wet?"

She only sighed in response.

"I guess I'll find out later, huh."

"What are you going to do?"

"I don't know. I'm not there yet. Right now I'm just picturing you naked against that steering wheel, your breasts pushed up against the gaps. Maybe I'm between your legs, licking you somewhere else too, and you're pushing against me so hard you don't care that you're also pushing the car's horn. Over and over and over."

It was a good thing she'd entered her condo's parking lot and that it was nearly empty, because she almost crashed after that. She turned off the ignition with shaking hands.

"Do you want me to carry you inside?" he asked.

"N-no. I think I'm going to need to walk for this."

And she did. She wondered how it was possible, for her legs to obey her mind, out the car, and into the elevator with Stephen so close, giving off such warmth she could imagine him glowing like something that had captured the sun.

She, on the other hand, felt so taut. If he touched her, she would vibrate and twang like a wire.

When he did, though—his fingers searching for her pulse, then gently skimming from wrist to her elbow—it was a curious feeling. How was it possible to be wound tight and yet still dissolve at the ends?

"Don't worry," he murmured as the elevator ascended. "I promise I'm going to make it good for you. I will make it so good."

She turned to him.

"I want it to be so good, it won't be a mistake," he said.

6

She wasn't lying when she said she lived in a studio.

It was dark when she let them in. She flicked a switch open, and soft, warm light oozed from the corners.

On any other day, Stephen would have paused to see just how an heiress—albeit a strange one, one trained by her father to be "normal"—lived. But this wasn't just any other day. Today, the heiress had her palms on his shoulders and then slowly coursed down his chest. She ran them up to push off his jacket, then down again to pull up his shirt. They slipped under and skimmed all over his body. He inhaled sharply and let her tug off his shirt.

Her eyes were heavy lidded. He could see the color flooding her cheeks and neck and lips, so full and round and parted.

"For a guy who isn't good with words, you know just what to say to me," she whispered, pulling him by the neck to crush her lips against his.

He wanted to play it cool, to let her explore and have her way with him, but when she kissed him like this, wild and on the edge of abandon, he just had to pull her body flush against his and kiss her back, deeply and dangerously. There was an elusive flavor in her mouth that teased him, and he swept his tongue, searching for it, maddened by it.

Somehow they were on the bed. She pulled off her top and he groaned at the sight of her bra. Lace, transparent white lace; her dark nipples framed by embroidered flowers. He bent over and placed his mouth over them, making good on the words he said in the car.

She was moaning now, and wriggling too. When his hands swept over all that glorious, golden skin and dipped to her hips, he found that she had gotten rid of her trousers. His hands drifted further, to the lace of her panties, and he lifted his head to say:

"God, yes...I was right. You're *dripping*."

She gasped and arched her neck, and so he kissed her there. He kissed her everywhere that he could see, consumed by a wild frenzy at how responsive she was, at the sounds he coaxed out of her. He loved how she pulled his hair and pushed her body against his, just like he hoped she would. And when he lost his pants and she touched him, up and down and tight, he felt so close to the edge, it didn't even occur that he should be cheering for himself.

There was only this moment and this girl.

"*Now*, Stephen," she commanded, but how could someone command and beg at the same time? He didn't hesitate to obey. There was the sound of a foil pack ripping, and a quick fumble, and then he was there. Deep inside her, moving in her. Kissing her, feeling her.

Loving her.

7

He was nuzzling her when she came to.

She stroked his hair and smiled. He was so funny. So sweet. His nose nudged into the space between her ear and jaw while his mouth dropped small, feather-light kisses on her neck.

"That was…" she sighed.

"Yeah."

"Yeah."

She turned to search his face, entangling their limbs further. The apology was gone from his eyes, replaced by satisfaction and amazement. She touched his cheek and kissed him on that adorable dimple.

"So," he cleared his throat. "Not a mistake?"

She shook her head and laughed.

They cuddled for what seemed like hours, hands still roaming, still exploring; no words exchanged except for the tiny sighs and little giggles that said so much more. But then Stephen rolled onto his back and his belly rumbled loudly.

"Shit," he said, pulling a pillow over his face as she laughed.

She sat and pulled him up. "Come on, Stephen Cruz.

Let's get something to eat."

She pulled on capris and a sweater as he struggled back into the clothes strewn all over her Moroccan-themed studio. "Nice place," he said drily. One of his shoes had ended up in the kitchenette.

They held hands in the elevator. She turned to the ground floor convenience store, but he said, "I know a better place," and led her away from the building.

They walked briskly in the cool, pre-dawn chill, past her street, lined with high-rise condominiums, into a busy road, then down another lined with hipster eateries and old buildings. They were now in what tourist books called Makati's heritage area—the grittier, colorful part of the city, where jeepneys rumbled at all hours. They had a brief glimpse of the flashing lights of the red light district, and then were in a narrow residential street that still had those funky, mezzanined '70s-era houses. Even a few trees.

Now they were among groups of people all walking towards the huge gray stone church at the corner of the street.

She raised an eyebrow, suddenly self-conscious of her running-to-the-convenience-store clothes and the fact that she couldn't remember the last time she'd been to church, let alone for *Simbang Gabi.* He shook his head and pointed instead at the row of open-air *carinderia* adjacent to the church walls.

"Don't freak out," he said, leading her to the middle stall. "They have the best *goto* here, believe me."

She let him order as she took her seat in one of the mint-green monoblock chairs on the sidewalk. The plastic table was covered by a salvaged bakery tarp. Over the air, broadcast through the church speakers, came the sound of bells, and then the low, intoning voice of the priest's homily.

He placed a small soda bottle and a bowl of thick rice porridge in front of her. The smell awakened her appetite—garlicky, gingery, and just a little bit gamey. She found a hard-boiled egg in her bowl and cut into its thick flesh, spooning it into her mouth with the salty, hot rice.

"Do you like it?" he asked.

"Yes."

He ate a few bites, and then: "Is this your first time in a *carinderia?*"

"Yes." She smiled tightly. "Did you bring me here to make a statement, Stephen?"

He stared at his bowl for a few long moments. "Cora...I knew who you were. Even before we talked. I saw your magazine cover earlier this morning. Yesterday morning, I mean."

She had another spoonful of *goto.* "I know," she sighed. "But you assumed I believed you when you pretended you had no idea who I was. I decided to go with it."

"What?"

"People will always make assumptions. I can either work with it or against it. I worked with it, this time." She ate a few more bites. "I'm glad I did."

"You are?" his eyes flooded with joy. He reached across the table for her hand. "Cora. I like you. I really do."

"I like you too, Stephen."

"Enough to keep seeing me?"

She smiled. "Yes."

"You're pretty sure about that."

She sat back in her seat. "If you think taking me into a *carinderia* is enough to turn me off, then you've sorely misjudged me, Stephen Cruz."

He shook his head. "God, no. I just...I thought you might want to try *goto,* that's all."

She laughed.

"I'm not going to lie, Stephen. I do want to keep seeing you. But it's not going to be easy. The *Tatler* cover was Dad's idea. My real debut, since he didn't see the point of one when I turned eighteen. From now until...until everything's settled, I'm going to be all out. My schedule's going to be crazy. I've been trying to learn all I can while Dad can still teach me, but now I'll be tested. Are you ready for that?"

He reached out to tuck a strand of hair behind her ear. "I'll find a way to manage it. It'll be like working with a giant Jenga puzzle."

She smiled and gripped his hand tight. "I have a feeling Dad will like you."

He smiled back. "Let's meet him."

She glanced at her watch. "Breakfast at seven sound good to you?"

He lifted his bottle of soda and clinked it against hers as the air filled with the sounds of Christmas carols. "Does he like *bibingka?* I know just the place."

THE END

ABOUT THE NEW EDITION

Well, I finally got around to it.

One Night At The Palace Hotel is my first steamy romance, and my first proper romance, really. It was finished in 2014 for the Buqo Steamy Reads workshop, and before that I'd been doing chick lit and YA. I thought it was fine, all things considered, but over the years, as I've re-read this story, well—it stood to be improved.

The head-hopping, for instance. *Oh God, the head-hopping.* I couldn't get rid of it without completely gutting and re-writing the story, so I just made it *clearer*, when it does happen, to hopefully minimize confusion. I know some of you have really been annoyed by this, and I'm sorry. I hope I've done better in my subsequent works.

The second and more important thing I've changed has to do with safe sex. I had a plot-related but ultimately misguided reason for why the scene was written the way it was written back in 2014, but I've since changed my mind. As a romance writer of sexy times, I have a responsibility to my readers to let you know that even being "crazed with lust" does not preclude practicing safe and responsible sex. So that part's been re-written.

Finally, over the years, people have written to find out what happens next with Sam and Consuelo. Fortunately, I addressed that with a cameo included in *One Night In The Streets of Makati*, a short story written for the

#romanceclass holiday anthology *Make My Wish Come True.* That story, which is about Consuelo's heiress best friend Cora and the 'regular guy' she meets, Stephen, has been added here. I hope you guys will enjoy the ending of Sam and Sue's story. Of course, now some people are asking me, 'What about Stephen and Cora?' and haha, yeah, I know—something new to work on!

ABOUT THE AUTHOR

Bianca Mori writes contemporary romances, romantic suspense, and crime fiction set in the Philippines, Europe, the United States, and all points in between. Her steamy stories have been called "fast-paced and super-hot," "engaging," "vivid," and "engrossing." She lives in Manila with her family and a hyperactive pug. Find Bianca on Facebook, Twitter, and Instagram as thebiancamori or at her website (www.biancamori.com).

OTHER WORKS BY THE AUTHOR

Search for these titles in your favorite ebook and paperback sources!

-Contemporary Romance -

Tame The Kitten
(Smashwords, Amazon, Spark Books paperback edition)
Girl gets off cab, biker nearly runs her over. Disaster…or the start of something sweet?

Chasing Waves
(Amazon, Paperback)
She's a single mom determined to finally be good—until she meets the Hot Training Manager who's supposed to whip her into shape.

-Romance/Suspense-

The Takedown Trilogy
(Amazon, Paperback)

Book 1: In Too Deep
Mary Shaw needs a vacation after a monster project. But a certain hottie's been following her around on this private island, and all is not what it seems…

Book 2: Peyton Riley
Peyton Riley is taken against her will by gorgeous crook Carson Varis to stop an art deal in Amsterdam. She learns that the rabbit hole is deeper than she suspects.

Book 3: Scorched Earth
Peyton Riley is on the run for her life. Can she takedown

the man who taught her everything she knows – and learn the truth about her bitter past?

-Crime-

Snakehead
(Amazon, Buqo, Paperback)
Where do you run when blood cannot be trusted?

-Anthologies-

Make My Wish Come True – A #romanceclass Christmas Anthology
Summer Feels – A #romanceclass anthology

11560366R00081

Printed in Great Britain
by Amazon